BATTLEFIELD GUARDIANS
ANGELS IN VIETNAM

Richard E. Warren

ISBN-13: 978-1722789800

ISBN-10: 1722789808

i

DEDICATION:

To John, Aubrey, and Annie

ABOUT THE AUTHOR

Richard "Rick" Warren is a father, grandfather, retired repairman, veteran, and thirty-year student of *The Urantia Book*. He is a fiction writer living in Fort Worth, Texas, USA. The "Battlefield Guardians" story was inspired by revelations in *The Urantia Book*, and created wholly by combining divine revelation with human imagination. It is the author's wish to provide a new vision of our next life; to make life on Earth richer in the knowledge and security of the persistence of eternal meanings and spiritual values; and to reveal the infinite possibilities and potentials of everlasting personal relationships with Our Creator and our fellows.

Editing & Formatting - Rick Lyon
Cover Design & Editing - Susan Lyon
Editing & Proofreading - James Woodward

battlefieldguardians.com

TABLE OF CONTENTS

Chapter 1

VIETNAM

Imagine landing at a military airport in a war zone at midday, on the equator, with eighty-eight other draftees. You disembark under full sun, no clouds. It's over a hundred degrees, and more humid than a greenhouse. Heat mirages appear in every direction. As you descend the mobile stairs a starched second lieutenant shouts, "Fall in!"

On the ground, the co-mingled smells of jet fuel, hot tarmac, and stale army fatigues filled our nostrils. We obediently formed four long columns beside the plane, a Pan Am Airlines jet. The ground heat quickly penetrated my boots.

The lieutenant marched us off the mushy-hot tarmac where we loaded onto deuce-and-a-half trucks. We rode a short way to the orientation tent, just a stone's throw from the South China Sea. Here the equatorial heat combined with green-tarp-tent smell and balmy ocean breeze.

After we filed into the large tent, standing at attention in front of folding chairs, a first sergeant mounted the foot-high stage and said, "At ease, men."

He began calmly and authoritatively, "Welcome to Chu Lai, Vietnam. This will be your home base for the next 365 days. Take your seat."

That was March 22, 1968, two months after the Tet Offensive, which turned out to be a pivot point in the Vietnam conflict. A pivot toward America's first military defeat.

Roll call began in alphabetical order. Soon enough my name came up.

"Baker, Ernie."

"Here, First Sergeant."

He had to be sixty years old. The heat didn't appear to

1

bother him in the least. Not a bead of sweat appeared on his face.

"You have CO status, Baker?"

"Yes, First Sergeant."

"Fall out, report to Headquarters. Colonel Simmons of second battalion will brief you."

"Yes, First Sergeant." It was embarrassing being singled out like that in front my fellow draftees.

A short stout corporal standing by the stage gave a follow-me sign. He led the way to a gigantic tent nearby, complete with concrete floor, a mess hall, open showers that could accommodate hundreds of soldiers, and partitioned offices. I followed the corporal to the battalion commander's office along one side of the tent. The clerk looked up and told us to go in. We stood at attention before the colonel's gray metal desk.

The corporal said, "Baker, the CO, sir," then handed him my orders and moved to the doorway remaining at attention.

The colonel looked up from his paperwork and said, "At ease."

"Baker, you're the first Conscientious Objector in my command. I'm not happy about it. You know you will still go out on patrol? And without any weapons? Others will be responsible for your safety? And this is an infantry unit that often finds itself in close combat?"

"Yes, sir."

"It's not too late to change your status, Baker."

"I know, sir. No, thank you." He looked at me disapprovingly then scanned my orders.

"I see here you're a nurse. You're now a medic in A company. Report to Captain Stone. Take him, Corporal."

"Yes, sir!" We three exchanged salutes, the corporal and I turned to leave.

"Baker, don't stir up trouble in my unit," barked the colonel before we were out the doorway.

"No, sir." I wondered what more trouble there could be in a war zone manned by unwilling draftees occupying a country in civil war.

Captain Stone's tent was much smaller. But like the others it had all side-flaps rolled up. The sound of gently crashing waves drifted in with the moist sea breeze.

"Sir. Baker, the CO."

"Thank you, Corporal."

"At ease, Private Baker."

He remained sitting, looking me over top to bottom.

"Straighten that gig line. This may be a war zone but you're still in the army, soldier."

"Yes, sir." I tucked in my fatigue shirt and lined up its buttons with my brass belt buckle.

"Why didn't you just get a deferment, Baker? You don't belong here."

"It was a mistake sir, I thought it was a world tour."

"Very funny, Baker. Hang on to that sense of humor, if you can."

"Yes, sir."

"You're now a medic assigned to first platoon. Corporal, get him gear and a med-pouch. Baker, you'll bunk with Lt. Smithson's platoon. Dismissed."

We came to attention, exchanged salutes and left to collect a set of gear: Two pairs of jungle boots, a rucksack, a steel-pot helmet with liner, two sets of jungle fatigues, three pairs of army green boxer shorts and socks, a medic's kit, three canteens, a rayon poncho, a flak jacket, an entrenching tool, a nylon tent with poles and stakes, a hammock, a month's supply of malaria pills, two plastic vials of mosquito repellent, a small bottle of salt tablets, and a duffel bag to stow it all.

I packed the duffel and shouldered the ruck. The corporal led the way and left me at the back of the orientation tent, never saying a word. I took a seat. The first sergeant was telling the assembled draftees about our "wily enemy." He went on for two hours about everything from foot fungus to court martials to booby traps and landmines, then dismissed us for chow. On the way out everyone checked a map on the bulletin board for the location of their assigned tent.

Eventually I found Lt. Smithson's tent. It had thirty bunks, fifteen on each side, all neatly made-up with camouflaged blankets stretched over white linen sheets. Rolled-up mosquito nets hung over each. Two corporals, the only ones there, sat on their bunks chatting. They stopped and looked me over.

One said, "Ah, you must be the objector. We heard you'd be arriving today to share our wretched little paradise here beside the South China Sea. Welcome O courageous one!" They both stood up, saluted, and bowed mockingly. "This is James of Thane, I'm Lawrence of Arizona. You have a first name?"

"Ernie."

Lawrence looked at my name tag with Baker printed in black ink and the single chevron on my sleeve. "Well, Private Ernie Baker, what brings you to this charming camp by the shores of Gitche Gloomy? Got tired of living?" He stuck out his hand and shook mine. James followed suit.

James asked, "Where you from?"

"Austin."

"So, you're used to the heat. You a nurse or something back in Texas?" he asked.

"Nurse."

"A male nurse. Just what we need here in tropical hell.

4

You'll get plenty of business experience what with the occasional disagreements we have discussing opposing ideologies with the Viet Cong," Lawrence quipped.

Just then a first lieutenant walked in; we snapped to attention. He looked at my nametag.

"At ease. Welcome Baker, I'm platoon leader. I don't have a problem with you being a CO. Keep your nose clean and we'll get on fine. You'll accompany me and these two when we go out in the field. Take that bunk." He pointed to a bed at the rear of the tent.

"Yes, sir."

"New orders, men. We air-lift out at 0630 hours tomorrow, the whole company. Inform the squad leaders when they show up." Lawrence and James replied with 'yes sirs.' He went to a small metal desk at the front of the tent and began writing.

Lawrence said, "Let's introduce the private to the mess hall, shall we, James?"

I put the gear under my bunk. We walked toward the gigantic tent on wooden pallets laid in the sand. These pallet paths connected all the tents.

"Where is Thane?" I asked.

"That's Lawrence's name for Scotland. We'd just immigrated a couple of years before the army called. My folks settled in New York, upstate."

"You both draftees?" I inquired.

Lawrence answered, "We are. I'm the platoon's artillery spotter, and James is the radioman. I have 301 days left, and James here has but 299. We showed up just in time for Tet. You heard of our recent war party, I presume?"

"It's the big news back in the States."

"How are things in the States?" Lawrence asked.

"War protests, campus and race riots. And Laugh-In."

"Laugh-In?" James asked.

"New TV comedy show; against the war."

"Hey, maybe the president will watch it and call off the war. The generals can learn to laugh instead of fight," Lawrence joked. "Maybe then I can go home, where the desert air is much more accommodating to my delicate complexion."

I liked these two. Lawrence was funny, and James was warm-hearted.

The mess hall was full. Hundreds of short-haired, fatigue-clad men, seated and in line, made a great din of chatter and clanking dinnerware. The air smelled of roast beef, potatoes, and baked buns.

Looking over this scene, I couldn't help wondering how many would die, be maimed, or psychologically wounded before their tour of duty was up. I recalled the news back home reporting a hundred or more were dying each week, with ten times that wounded.

We stood in line, loaded our trays, then took a seat and ate without saying much. Too noisy to talk.

After the meal James and Lawrence wanted to go to the USO for ice cream and a beer. The long trip on the plane had zapped my energy—that and the tropical heat. I begged off and caught a nap on my bunk.

I woke at sunset when a rowdy group with a boombox arrived at the tent. The "Eve of Destruction" was playing. I slipped out, walked toward the beach and sat on a pile of plump sandbags. I thought about the year ahead living and working in a war zone. It hit me how different Vietnam is from the safety and comfort of the States, and how much I would miss seeing Karen. She was probably just starting her day at art school.

It was about midnight when I got back to the tent, but sleep wouldn't come. The rest of the night I lay awake. My mind went on and on about everything from the war to the meaning of life. Around dawn, when there was enough light, I wrote a short letter to Karen, telling her about the first day in Nam.

At sunrise, reveille blew over the camp speakers. I was amazed by how hot it was already. We had a quick breakfast after which the whole company was ordered to gather supplies, pack our rucksacks, and fill our canteens. I had time to mail the letter at company HQ before we were put on trucks and taken to a nearby helipad.

We loaded onto more than a dozen helicopters, eight men and their fully packed rucks on each. All the choppers had fifty caliber machine guns, one mounted and manned on each side. The flock took off all at once. The roar was spine-tingling, and the fear was palpable.

Chapter 2

FIRST MISSION

"We're probably going in hot," one of the pilots yelled as we approached our destination. Soon small arms fire could be heard over the helicopter noise. Several rounds clunked against the skin of our chopper. Both machine gunners looked for rifle smoke and began spitting out fire in that direction. The pilots slammed the birds down in flat, dry rice paddies. We jumped off, hitting the ground and crouching behind short paddy dikes. Bullets were zizzing everywhere. The chopper blades whipped the air hard lifting off, trying to get away quickly. I looked up to see two of them blowing smoke trails. A minute later one crashed near the horizon with a great boom. I was shaking.

"Form a perimeter!" Captain Stone commanded over the radio. Crawling on bellies and leaping over dikes, each platoon took a position making a rough circle. Riflemen and grenadiers fired as they advanced and kept firing once in place.

"Medic!" someone yelled. There were four medics in the company, one with each platoon. I was closest. Rounds were coming in and going out in every direction. Was I supposed to get up and run to the wounded man? I did. God only knows why I wasn't hit. The man lay twisted on his side. He wasn't moving. I felt his neck for a pulse. His eyes were open and fixed, pupils fully dilated.

"He's gone," I said. A round had penetrated his helmet; a pool of blood soaked the ground under his head.

The soldier who had called for a medic was hysterical. "Don't die!" he said repeatedly, looking at his dead buddy's face.

Lawrence yelled "Baker! Over here!" I crouched as I ran back. Lt. Smithson was hit in the left foot and bleeding badly. As we lay low, bullets continued zinging overhead. I removed his bloody boot; he was missing the end of the third toe. I nervously

8

trimmed off dangling skin and dug a bandage out of the med pouch, wrapping it tightly to stop the bleeding. The pain had to be excruciating, but he didn't say anything.

I informed him about the dead man and asked, "You want morphine?"

"No. Gimme that mic!" James crawled to Smithson and handed over the radio's microphone at the end of a coiled cord. He called for artillery, a locator smoke round. "Charlie Zulu, send a red round."

Lawrence yelled out the coordinates. The lieutenant repeated them into the mic. Thirty seconds later a locator round landed in front of our platoon, about a hundred yards outside the perimeter. Red smoke went up.

Some of the enemy fire was coming from a long bamboo hedgerow in front of our platoon. Lawrence used the radio to walk the rounds toward it. That was followed by jets dropping napalm and thousand-pound bombs. We kept as low as possible behind the dikes. The explosions were deafening, and the napalm created great fireballs. Bomb shrapnel ripped the air, black smoke went up in great plumes. Enemy fire quickly diminished. I discovered the enemy AK47 rifles sounded very different from the US weapons. They made a distinct popping noise. Finally, it stopped and only our weapons could be heard.

"Cease fire!" Captain Stone ordered over the radio. Seconds later the artillery stopped, and the jet bombers disappeared.

"Good job, Lawrence," Smithson said.

Now the silence was deafening. There was hardly a sound for a brief moment. The enemy was in retreat; we glimpsed several slipping away into dense brush and tall, thick hedgerows.

Smithson said to James, "Get a medivac in here to move that dead hero and the wounded out. And bring me his left boot."

9

James hurriedly called the rear for a medical chopper.

"Tighten the perimeter! And bring your wounded to first platoon's position," Captain Stone ordered over the radio from his position at the perimeter's center. Some men scrambled to connect the company in an unbroken circle covering several rice paddies while others brought injured ones to where the dead man was. I went for the boot.

A few minutes later the captain called for the platoon leaders. The lieutenant dug in his ruck for a clean sock, then put it on and quickly laced up the dead man's boot. He ran crouching and limping toward Stone's position, trying to ignore his wounded toe.

"What now?" I asked Lawrence.

"Patrols probably," he answered, taking off his rucksack. It must have weighed 90 pounds. Mine did too. I had to carry three spare battery packs for James' radio since I had no rifle or pistol. We all carried enough rations and supplies for two weeks, including our pup-tents, ponchos, air mattresses, and personal effects. Everyone except me had to tote weapons and abundant ammo, including grenades and Claymore mines.

"You feeling a bit queasy, Private Ernie?" Lawrence asked with genuine concern. I was still shaking after that intense half hour—after watching the chopper crash and then seeing the dead man. In my short nursing career I had seen death, but not by violence, and not one so young. His frozen expression stuck in my mind, along with the terrified face of his buddy. I couldn't help thinking that his life, his youth, was squandered in one terrifying moment on this nameless rice paddy. And his family wouldn't even know it for days.

"Wanna give up being a CO?" Lawrence said, offering me his 45-caliber sidearm.

I shook my head and asked, "Aren't we supposed to go after the enemy? Isn't that what the army is out here to do?"

"No, they're dispersed by now, hiding in the bushes, local

10

farms, and villages," James answered. He saw I was still trembling. "You'll be all right, Ernie," he added kindly, peering into my sweaty, no-doubt fearful face.

Nothing was said or done for a few minutes, until the lieutenant loped back to our position. By then I'd taken some deep breaths and calmed down a bit.

"The company is splitting up. First platoon will set up basecamp on that hill." The lieutenant pointed to a high, lone mound rising out of the flat plain, about two kilometers away. "First platoon squad leaders!" he yelled. Four men ran toward us, crouching and carrying their weapons but not their rucks.

"Tell your men we'll set up base on that hill tonight. C squad will walk point," Smithson ordered. "My team will follow C, then A, B, and D squads. Wait for my order to move out."

"Yes, sir," they replied in harmony and ran back to their squads to relay the plan.

Just then the medivac landed and quickly loaded six bandaged and wounded ones plus the fallen man, a boy really. I urged Lieutenant Smithson to leave and get his toe treated properly. He refused. The chopper took off raising a small dust storm out of the dry paddy.

"Prepare to move out!" Smithson shouted after the bird lifted off. As we were leaving, Captain Stone took a small group outside the perimeter to count the enemy dead, seizing their weapons and personal belongings.

"First platoon, let's move, and stay spread out!" Smithson commanded. We marched single file to the designated hill, without incident until almost there.

Someone at the front of the column yelled, "VC!" and pointed to two people in black silk pajamas running away, about three-hundred meters off our left flank. They were wearing conical straw hats and carrying rifles. They disappeared into a thick row of tall bamboo growing out of a three-foot sodden dike.

11

"Keep in line!" Smithson ordered, looking through binoculars. "Could be an ambush." We proceeded to the hill. We were soaked with sweat by the time we reached the top. I could see the pain in the lieutenant's face—his toe was hurting. He yelled, "Check for mines before you take a position."

Everyone walked around gingerly searching the ground for freshly disturbed dirt and trip wires. Mines, I learned, were a soldier's greatest hazard, and his worst fear.

Discarded ration cans and army trash was scattered around. Obviously, this hill had been used many times. After a thorough search Smithson ordered, "Dig in, men. And don't use the old foxholes!" There were a dozen or more well-dug holes around the hilltop.

"Why can't we use the holes that are dug?" I asked James and Lawrence.

"The VC put booby traps and punji sticks in them," James answered.

The platoon spent the rest of the day digging three-foot holes in the hard, dry, red ground. Then before dark, James, Lawrence, and I set up our mosquito-proof nylon tents not far from the lieutenant, near the center of the barren hilltop. He called the squad leaders to arrange rotating night watch and to impart the plan for the next day. I was exempted from watch since I carried no weapon.

By the time we were set up the sun was almost gone. In the twilight, we sat in small groups for a meal, warming our rations in canteen cups over hexamine heat tablets.

The lieutenant limped around the hilltop checking on everyone while we three sat together and talked.

"Did you know that kid who was killed," I asked, as the stinky fumes from the smoldering tablets rose around us.

"He was from Alaska. Arrived last month," James said. "Drafted after his first year of college. He was dismissed for low grades. He was funny, called himself, 'a failed freshman.' Everyone liked him right away."

"The cream of America," Lawrence added, "His blood spilt here 8,000 miles from home. Such is war." And then somewhat sarcastically, "You made out your will yet, Private Baker?"

"Sure. Like you, we had to name a beneficiary on some form just before we left the States."

"It's a lottery for life, this war thing," Lawrence said wistfully.

"It seems like such a waste of life. You guys are used to it already, aren't you?"

"Numbed to it maybe," James answered. "Everybody just wants to do their time and get home in one piece."

"The news back home publishes the body count every week, ours and theirs," I said. "It didn't really hit me until today, what that means. Do you think the war will end soon? The president and the Pentagon keep saying we're winning."

"Ha! After Tet we all realized our charming, clever, tenacious enemy isn't about to give up. And if I know the army, it won't give up either, no matter how many young and unwilling draftees like ourselves America puts on the ground. The people of South Vietnam just won't accept our gracious proffer of a puppet government. Would you?" Lawrence asked with irony.

"So, young boys like that one today are dying needlessly? Is that it? We're just as likely to die as him, aren't we?" I said with dismay and rising indignation. "Aren't you guys mad? I may be new but it's obvious this war is wrong. Surely you see that, you know that. So I have to wonder what keeps you fighting?"

"Fighting? We aren't fighting are we, James? We just take orders. It's that or move into the army's one-star hotel and chain gang at Fort Leavenworth, Kansas. Maybe you'd have us follow your lead and become objectors. Not a bad idea, now that I mention it."

James replied with touching honesty, "I actually thought about being a CO, after I finally figured out that the war just isn't right. But my dad fought with Britain in World War II, and he raised me to be a fighter for freedom, to be a brave soldier like he was. We argued a lot about Vietnam before I got drafted. I knew it would kill him to have an objector for a son. I guess I figured since he lived through four years of combat, I could at least try to make it through one. I'm just glad I didn't sign up as a volunteer. The draft means only two years in the army. About a year in training and one in Nam, and I'm done."

"But is your heart in it?" I felt compelled to ask.

"No, not really. If it ever was, it's not anymore."

"How about you, Lawrence?"

"No one's heart is in it after Tet, except the generals. And truth be told, they're probably just following orders like us lowly ground pounders."

"That's crazy, isn't it?" I said, feeling more angry.

"Crazy is another name for war, Private Ernie," Lawrence answered. "You'll get used to it. Anyway, the beast in us has to spill some blood every few years or we start feeling civilized. You wouldn't want that."

"Might be worth a try," I replied, then asked, "You sound cynical. Are you?"

He looked at me and after a moment said, "Cynicism gives good cover for fear and anger, I guess."

As we chatted, darkness closed in and the stars came out in remarkable brilliance. There was no moon that night and the only light in the area was an occasional cigarette being lit behind cupped hands. We stared up at the Milky Way. It was starrier than I'd ever seen. It looked like a giant rip in the cosmos, a great tear in the sky. I couldn't help wondering if there were other inhabited worlds, and whether there were soldiers on those worlds watching the silent sky and thinking about the comforts of home and the insanity of war. As we watched the starry ceiling above, a soft chorus of crickets suddenly sang out.

We were absorbed in the moment until James asked, "You think there is life around other stars, life like ours? I used to lie out under the night sky at home and try to imagine what it would be like on another planet. I figured if a planet is big, the extra gravity would make the people short and stout. If a planet is small, they are tall. And maybe they could jump fifty feet."

"You guys hear about NASA planning to land on the moon next year?" I asked.

Lawrence replied, "Yeah, we have to beat the Ruskies there, don't we?! Exciting stuff. Let's volunteer, James. Be better than humping our rucks and dodging bullets here in Southeast Asia for the next ten months. You can join us, Objector Ernie. You don't seem to have an affinity for war, even though you've only been here two days. Very judgmental of you I might add. Give it some time, you'll learn to loathe it."

"What's on the moon? Maybe creatures who can live without air, beings who live off space energy," James speculated. "They probably look down and wonder if there's life on Earth. If they have brains like ours, they must wonder what's going on in the rest of the universe like we do."

"You guys think much about the meaning and purpose of life? You face death every day. You must have given some thought to it," I said.

Lawrence quickly answered, "Sure, I think of it all the time." Then he paused. "James can tell you, my preferred persona is that of a philosopher. It is my chosen service and solemn duty to this benighted world, to explain the universe and the reason we find ourselves in these flesh and bone bodies on this tiny speck of a planet floating in time and space." We had to laugh at the pompous way he said it, like he was an indisputable oracle of esoteric information from on high.

"Do tell," said James. "Here he goes with the deep-thinking stuff. Tell Ernie how long you've been a philosopher."

"Oh, since about age seven. One day while on a bike ride by a river in the woods, I had a vision. I came home and told my parents I was going to be a holy man and lead the world to Truth. Dad said, 'Good! Begin by doing your homework.' Mom smiled kindly and added, 'I had a vision too, when you were in the womb, that you would become a great philosopher. Now go do your homework so you can get a good job. Philosophers are poor and we may need you to take care of us when we're old, feeble, and cranky. You'll need a paying skill.' It was disappointing. But now, here I am, making an astounding four hundred bucks a month as a soldier in a glorious war halfway 'round the world. No doubt they're proud and feeling secure about their old age."

"I do wonder whether there is anything after dying, especially on days like today when someone is killed," said James thoughtfully. "That's the fourth man I've seen die in my two months here. None of us knows if there'll be a tomorrow. A mortar round could land on our heads in ten minutes. I like to believe this is not all there is. But if our body is killed, what's left? What does the philosopher say about that, Lawrence?"

"James, James. Fret not, my brother. Your essence is unkillable. That was the message I received on the bike ride! We aren't just soulless animals; we have an infinite and eternal essence at our core. Most don't know it but we are Godlings."

"Wish I'd gotten such a message," James said. "How can you be sure a seven-year old's vision is true or valid?"

"Don't doubt it, my man. It's far better to believe there's life after life. Makes this world a little more bearable."

After hearing that, I had to ask Lawrence, "You think religion has it right? Seems like they all promise soul survival in some form."

"They do. And this is where wisdom comes in. Philosophy takes the insights of religion and the facts of science and formulates a coherent vision of reality. Science reveals the nature of the Earth and the stars, and the working of our bodies, all that is the outer physical realm. Religion reveals the inner realm, our souls and our destiny, the spiritual arena."

"You really *are* a philosopher," James declared. "So, you're saying there is a God?"

"I'm saying the existence of personality means there has to be an original personality, one who started it all." Lawrence pointed to the sky, "Somewhere out there in the cosmos there is an Original Person. And somewhere inside, at our core, there exists that same personal reality. God—for lack of a better word."

That set James and me thinking. Nothing was said for a minute. I could faintly hear other conversations and occasional laughs from the rest of the platoon spread around the hill in two and three-man groups.

"So, if there is a God, what do you guys think the purpose of life is? And why all the suffering?" James pondered. "I've been asking people that all my life, including preachers and priests. Only a few of them have a believable answer. And none of them agree much."

"Good questions, thoughtful Thane," Lawrence said. "Surely life, with its joys and its suffering must have some meaning, value, or purpose. What say you, Ernie the Objector?"

"I know there has to be more to life than what we see."

"Ah so! You have rightly discerned the truth, Private Baker. Plato suggested humanity attempts to discern the meaning of life by observing shadows cast by unseen creators. Of course, the Bard of Avon made a salient point when he had Hamlot declare, 'There are more things in Heaven and Earth, Horatio, than are dreamt of in your philosophy.'"

James immediately asked, "Why is it, figuring out the meaning and purpose of life is so hard? Most people don't get Plato or know Shakespeare. There's no map or handbook. We just wander around the planet like everything is normal. What is really going on? If God exists, why can't we see God?"

"Another excellent question, James. There was a beaucoup savvy French philosopher 400 years ago who stated the answer so very elegantly and succinctly. He wrote: 'Human beings must be known to be loved; but divine beings must be loved to be known.' Ponder that during our next firefight," Lawrence grinned. "The meaning, value, and purpose of life are self-evident to deep-thinking minds. But who has time to spend exploring the depths of an invisible and inscrutable Providence when we could be fighting with our visible enemies, those with whom we disagree to the point of homicide?"

"By Providence, you mean God, right?" asked James.

"God has to be. As I intimated before, James, it makes sense that the creator of personality is at least a person, even THE person. Somewhere in the universe there exists that First Person, the Creator of All. Think of this person as unique in all the vast cosmos, the only one who has no parent, an originator of all things and beings. But, add to that thought the insights from many a deep-thinking internal explorer. Ones who dotted our history—the sages, prophets, and philosophers. Their consensus is that not only is there a First Person, an uncaused cause of all subsequent causes, but that our essence—who we really are—must be of and from that Person. They all tend to agree God is within, as well as without."

"That's a leap," I said, "but it lines up with what I've felt before. Maybe that's just intuition. I do feel sure there's something bigger, something greater going on, but I never could have put it into words like you just did."

James scratched his chin stubble thoughtfully. "I don't know. If God really is within, why do we act like animals? Are you saying God is part animal?"

"I'm saying we inherited these animal bodies from our parents, and they from theirs. But being an animal is just the starting point, a temporary state. We philosophers say there exists the possibility that the animal in us can be subjugated, that the divine essence can come forth, given proper conditions.

18

That, my friends, is the purpose of life, self-realization of inherent divinity."

"What 'proper conditions?'" James asked.

"Ah, now we're drilling down to the nitty and the gritty, James," Lawrence said with a professorial tone. "The physical world demands that, in order to live, we must breathe, eat, and rest. Add in procreation to fulfill the innate drive to survive in and through our offspring. A dog doesn't have the conceptual framework to ask, 'Is there more than air, food, sleep, and mating?' The dog doesn't even connect the act of sex with reproduction. But the human does. The reasoning human mind asks, 'What is the purpose of breathing, eating, sleeping, and making more humans?' We humans have the capacity to evaluate the quality of our thoughts and our acts. Animals do not. Humans, if we dare, think not only about survival, but survival after death. As our brother Ernie pointed out: something tells us that what our senses perceive is not all there is. Our thoughts, which always precede our acts, can bring about the right conditions for understanding, enlightenment, and spiritual expansion. What are you two thinking of now?"

James answered, "Just what we're talking about, whether I will survive when I die."

I said, "I was wondering exactly what survives when my body and brain die?"

"Excellent, Private Baker. The philosopher's answer to your query is: Nothing good dies, the only things of lasting value are values themselves. The religionist would answer it is your soul that survives, and that the substance of the soul is divine values. All religions worthy of the name teach that humans have souls. And that soul consists of spiritual values, transcendent values generally defined under the three-fold heading of truth, beauty, and goodness. The truth-seeking scientist, if he or she is completely honest and objective, says, 'There is much we do not know.' The atheistic scientist, of course, is a slave to reason, to the senses, to what can be observed experimentally. The atheist cannot abide spiritually based values, including the soul, because the soul can't be proven or quantified."

He went on, "The spiritual experimenters of the East and the West, those mystics who dare to explore the inner life, almost all report that humans not only possess a soul, but also have a fragment of divinity which resides within. When an Eastern guru greets you with the word, 'Namaste,' he is saying 'The God in me salutes the God in you.' Jesus clearly stated, 'the kingdom of God is within.' To further answer your question about conditions, look inside. It was good advice that great teacher gave: 'Knock and the door will be opened.' The universe is designed so that the sincere desire to know about the meaning, purpose, or value of life is enough to bring forth the teacher. And the teacher can take many forms."

That was the deepest conversation I'd ever had about the meaning of life and whether there was an afterlife. I never forgot it and often pondered Lawrence's philosophical insights. He belonged in a university, not a war. What a waste if he should die on the battlefield.

Then James wanted to talk about home, to know more about the latest happenings, about Martin Luther King's marches, the hippie movement, resistance to the draft, recent movies, and other news of the day. I told them everything I could remember after which we inflated our air mattresses and prepared to sleep. It was a beautiful night, much cooler, and there was enough breeze to keep the mosquitoes away.

Lying there beside my tent, looking up at the Milky Way I thought, "This is the same sky as back home." Such a strange juxtaposition, the cosmic field of beauty above, and this field of danger and ugly death on the ground. It took a long while to get to sleep. I kept thinking of how close death and injury had come earlier that day, and Lieutenant Smithson's toe stump. It would need a fresh bandage in the morning.

Chapter 3

A PLACE OF REVELATION

It must have been after midnight. I was startled awake when someone on guard shouted in a panic, "Incoming!" I sat bolt upright and heard several thunks. Basic training taught us that's the sound mortars make when they are launched. I leapt from the air mattress into my foxhole. The first mortar landed half way up the hill. The next one a little higher, and the third landed smack on top, not far away. I crouched as low as possible wishing I could crawl into my helmet.

Several more struck. I heard a cry for a medic. Before I could get out and find the med pouch, a mortar exploded next to my foxhole. The concussion wave from it was tremendous. Suddenly there was a floating sensation. I looked down and saw my body slumped inside the foxhole. It was very odd rising above everything. But I felt no pain, in fact it was freeing in a way. I could still see and hear the chaos on the ground, there was yelling, and James was calling artillery for illumination rounds. But I was above it and rising quickly. Then, everything faded to black.

The next thing I recall was seeing two luminous beings, peering intensely at me. One of them said quite distinctly, "You are all right, Ernie."

"What? I died?" the words barely came out, like a muffled whisper.

The other being said, "No." They both had brilliant and kindly faces. Their voices were as soft as a rose petal.

"You are alive," the first one assured me.

I took a long look at them. "You are beautiful."

"Thank you," the second one replied with a dazzling and charming smile.

"Who are you?"

"We are your Guardians," said the first.

"Guardians? Wait... I didn't die and I'm alive?"

"Yes. Don't you feel alive?" answered the second.

After a moment, I said, "I must be... But this could be a dream."

"Not a dream, Ernie," the first said firmly.

"The mortar, it exploded. I was hurt and floated over everything."

"Your body was injured but not destroyed. This is not a dream, a hallucination, or an illusion," the second being declared with an undeniable confidence.

"Is this heaven?" I asked. "You know my name. But who are you?"

The first one repeated, "We are your Guardians. You may call me Joyah, and this is Rayah. We are of an angelic order. We have been assigned to your watch-care and education."

I tried to shake off a foggy feeling. "Guardians?"

"Yes, we are your Guardian Angels."

"Were you with me when the mortar hit?"

"We were," Joyah replied.

"I'm not understanding, I'm sorry... You're saying my body is alive, but I'm not in it? And I'm not dead?"

"That is correct," Rayah said with absolute conviction and authority.

"How can that be? Where is this? Where are we? If you're really guardians, why was I hurt?"

Joyah answered in a touching and reassuring tone, "Ernie, the attachment to your flesh and bone body has been severed, but only temporarily. We are in what you might refer to as a holding area, a place of revelation above the Earthly realm and below what you would conceive to be the heavenly realm. I assure you, there is a reason you are here. You may be certain that your Earthly body was not fatally injured, and you will soon return to it."

"So, you're telling me a person can exist without a body? And where we are is half-way to heaven?"

"You may think of it that way," replied Rayah. "And as Joyah said, this is a place of revelation, of education. It is not a place of permanent residence. You are here for a purpose and will very soon re-enter your physical body. Your life on Earth is not yet over."

"What purpose? I am not understanding. This is too much to believe. There was an explosion by my foxhole; I left my body; consciousness faded. Then I woke up here with you two, and you're telling me I'm not dead... and that I'm going to return to my body?"

For the first time, I took note of the surroundings. I had a body of sorts. It looked just like Joyah and Rayah's, solid but light. I had arms, legs and a trunk. I squeezed each of my arms and touched my face with both hands. I couldn't quite decide whether I was solid or light. There was nothing to see but the three of us. Everything beyond us was silent and indistinct, misty-like. Neither could I understand whether we were standing or floating. But I did feel painless, safe, and good.

"Your mortal senses will be limited during your short time here, Ernie, but other senses will be enhanced," Rayah informed me.

"Short time? How long? If this is really real, what exactly am I doing here?"

Joyah answered, "We have but a few minutes more. Here you will discover many things. We do truly want to help you understand what has happened. And there is a reason you are here. We require your help."

"My help? What could I possibly do for angels, assuming you exist and this is real? I still don't understand how I can be alive here—and there. You're telling me my body is still alive down there, and I'm going back. I have to be dreaming, or... or that blast is making me hallucinate. That has to be it!"

"Where you are, what you are seeing, hearing, and feeling is more real than what you saw, heard, and felt in your material body," Joyah stated with total assurance. Something in me wanted to believe her.

She went on, "We have an assignment that involves you. The explosion provided an opening, an opportunity for a first meeting. Your appearance here coincides with our assigned task. We are hoping that you will cooperate, that you will volunteer to help us complete our assignment at subsequent meetings."

"Assignment? Subsequent meetings? What assignment? What do angels have to do with me, what are you saying!?" I was feeling slightly frustrated.

Rayah answered in an understanding tone, "Our mission, our assignment, involves revelation. If you agree—and you must know that you are not obliged to cooperate with us—we want you to deliver a message to your world about life after life in the flesh, about the worlds above, the heavens, as you call them."

"Revelation? You're saying there is an afterlife? There is heaven? If there is, why would you choose me to reveal it? I'm not a religious person. And why have you not shown yourselves before?"

Without the least impatience, Rayah explained, "There most assuredly is an afterlife. And there are heavens that human imagination cannot conceive, glorious and divine. But because we are invisible to human eyes here on Earth, we do not make direct physical contact, except in emergencies. Angels are constantly watching over you and your fellows during life in the flesh. And even though we Guardians are not permitted to show ourselves, we can and sometimes do, save you. But almost always in a way that can't be seen or proven. Life on Earth is designed to elicit and promote faith. And what humans sometimes believe is miraculous is often merely Guardian Angels performing invisibly."

"You seem sincere and for some crazy reason I want to believe you. But I'm still doubting this is actually real, this... this place, and you two. Right now, I'm remembering stories of dying or injured people being taken up and seeing visions of higher worlds. Maybe that's what's going on."

"We hope you can be convinced of the reality of this experience, Ernie," Joyah said. "And doubt not, many of those stories you heard are based in fact, although some are distorted by erroneous human interpretations and the inherent limitations of mortal understanding. What you are experiencing here and now is real. And what we are asking of you, we ask in sincerity. Our mission to reveal certain facts to you has been approved by our supervisors. You can perform a great service to the people of your world. If you will only consent."

"Consent? How can I give consent when I'm not even sure you exist, or that this is real?" They smiled at me so tenderly and earnestly; I will never forget that smile. "I do have to say, this does *feel* real. But I remember dreams that felt real, until I woke up."

"Do you recall ever wondering if you were in a dream while you were in it?" Rayah asked.

"No, I guess not... No, I don't. And my dreams are almost always strange and disjointed."

"Does this place have that same feel, that same essence the disordered dream state has?"

"No," I had to admit. "There's something very real about this, and you. I can't explain it. In fact, it's starting to feel more real than life down there."

25

Then Joyah said, "Maybe speaking with someone you know will help with your doubt. Allow us to introduce loved ones you knew as a child, and who you often thought of after they departed Earth."

Out of the pale blue mist that surrounded us, two familiar faces appeared. I knew them but couldn't quite put a name to them.

The Guardians must have sensed the absence of recognition because Rayah said, "Ernie, surely you recall your Nana and Grandad?"

I was stunned for a long moment. But then realized it had to be them. "Nana? Grandad? How can it be you?" I asked, but somehow knew, it was them when we locked eyes. "You look so young!" They moved close and hugged me, the feeling of familiarity was unmistakable; I knew that embrace. Suddenly I felt like crying and blurted out, "I missed you! You're alive?"

"We are, Ernie," Nana said in a voice that was undoubtedly hers. Their young faces were beaming with joy and bright smiles.

"So good to see you grandson," Grandad said. "We look forward to the day the whole family has its next reunion." Reunions were annual events in our family.

"It really is you. I can't believe it. What? How? You..." I was overwhelmed with feelings that harkened to the days of their deaths. I reached out, took them in my arms, and squeezed them. We all laughed, and I knew then I wasn't dreaming. That embrace was more real than any I'd ever had. "You are so beautiful, and young!"

"Eternity has its rewards, Ernie," Nana said. "When you die, you'll get a new body, kind of like these." She gestured to their forms."

I hardly knew how to react. "I'm so amazed by all of this, and so happy to see you two again. And I'm beginning to believe this is not a dream or a hallucination. These Guardians say my body is not dead and I will go back to it. Do you know these angels?"

"We do," Grandad replied. "They contacted us the minute you were brought to this place, requesting that we greet you."

"How long have you been alive? I mean, where do you live now? Who else is there? What's it like? Is that where I'll go when I die?" Questions were flooding my mind now that doubts were fading.

Then Joyah said, "Answers to those and many other questions involve our assignment, Ernie. We want to answer them. It is part of our work."

"But, I can't stay here, can I?"

"We are hoping that you will cooperate, that you will volunteer to help us complete our assignment at subsequent meetings. You should know there are others in similar situations—ones who have come here, been given a view of the next life, and returned to report what they learned. This is what we are doing, Ernie," Rayah explained.

She added, "You are still young and could have many years ahead in which to assimilate what we reveal, and then share it with your Earthly peers. Seldom do we see one of your age with such a compassionate heart. It was noted when you decided not to kill in your military service. And this rare compassion was first confirmed when you chose to become a healer. We well know that was not an easy decision for you. You've suffered much ridicule for taking a role that is normally relegated to females. These choices were for the right reasons— because you care about the health and welfare of others. There is no higher form of love." That was very gratifying to hear, but I still wasn't clear about what they were proposing.

"So, what do you want me to do exactly? I'm a nurse, not a teacher or a preacher."

Joyah said, "We are hoping that this experience, and more to come, will inspire you to greater service. That you will write down everything that has happened here, and everything that we reveal in the future. That you will, in due time, publish these revelations. Very soon we will make contact again. Indeed, this process will require many sessions and much revelation. But you should not doubt that we will continue to be your faithful Guardians on Earth, as well as your teachers from on high. We will be your willing and able supporters in this revelatory project."

"I see... and when do you want to start? What about my body back down there? How am I supposed to return to it? And when?"

"We will return you to the material world soon enough," Rayah answered. "Now that your doubts have been removed, we know that you will retain memories of us, your grandparents, and this meeting."

"Just when I was beginning to like being here, I have to go."

Joyah put a comforting hand on my shoulder and said, "You will want to bid your grandparents good-bye for a season. But, to be sure, you will rejoin them, and many others, when you resurrect." I remember feeling a deep resonance with that word, resurrect.

Rayah added, "We know it is difficult to return after you have had a taste and a vision of life beyond. But now you know, and may be sure, that we are always at your side. And even though we cannot be seen or heard with your human senses, we will be in contact, much as we are now." I trusted what she said, and my grandparents gave an approving smile. Just then I felt a powerful longing to stay. But I knew the right thing to do was to follow the angels' words.

"So long, Nana, Grandad. I love you, and I'm very glad to know you're alive. And so young!" We three hugged again and they looked me in the eye. Nana said, "We love you, Ernie. And we'll be there when you're done on Earth."

That's everything I could recall.

Chapter 4

RETURN TO DUTY

"Private Baker, can you hear me?" All I could see was the face of a woman. Then I noticed the silver lieutenant's bar on the collar of her army green fatigue shirt. My hearing was off but I heard her question. I tried to respond.

"Yes," I whispered.

"We're going to take care of you," she said.

"Where...?"

"You're in Da Nang hospital. You were injured in the field." Another person moved in close, a male, also in fatigues. I recognized his captain's bars and the caduceus pin on his collar.

"Rest easy, soldier," he said. "You're going to be all right. How many fingers do you see?"

"Three, sir."

"Good. Just relax, we'll get you cleaned up and moved to a bed soon. Apparently, a concussion knocked you out. We don't see any wounds. Does your head hurt?" he asked.

"Yes, sir." It was pounding. It felt like my brain was too big for my skull.

"You're going to be all right in a few days," he said, and then went to another injured soldier lying on a litter. It dawned on me this was a triage tent.

"You'll be OK, don't worry," the nurse assured me with a warm and comforting smile. "Aides! Move this man to C Ward," she called out. Two smiling Vietnamese men in US army fatigues moved me onto a gurney and took me to a bed in an adjacent tent with many other wounded. It was either before sunup or after sundown—I wasn't sure—only that it was twilight.

Another nurse met us at the ward's entrance. "You're

29

going to be just fine. Do you want to contact your family, soldier?" she asked while writing on a clipboard. It was hard to hear, like she was speaking softly.

"I'm not sure. Seems like I'm all right, except hearing and a headache."

"Your chart says you got a concussion. But we better get X-rays. Looks like there was some bleeding from your ears."

"Your hearing should clear up in a few days. You rest, I'll get some of that blood out."

"Do you know if others were hurt?" I asked.

"I don't. What's your unit? I'll see if any of them are here." I gave her my unit number. She left and returned with a tray of warm sterilized cloths and swabs. Suddenly I remembered the encounter with the Guardians, and my grandparents. I had an urge to tell her but decided not to. She might think I was raving. Besides, talking made my head hurt more.

She went to work on my ears. "Where you from, Private Baker? Your dog tags say you're a CO, probably a medic, right."

"Yes. From Austin. You?"

"Philly. And I'll be returning there in a few days, Lord willin' and the world doesn't end." She finished cleaning my ears and said, "You take it easy. Get some sleep, OK? I'll check and see if any of your buddies are here." She then turned to a badly wounded man in the next bed. He was calling out a woman's name. I thought of my family and whether to tell them about being injured. I decided not to. It would only cause worry.

I was in the ward three days. The X-rays didn't find other injuries. I was able to move around after the first day, to go to the latrine alone, though my head throbbed at first. This gradually diminished and hearing got better each day. At one point a hearing specialist came by and dug around in both ears to remove the remaining dried blood and dirt. That felt better and improved hearing a lot. He did a test and said some high frequency hearing was permanently lost. What hearing remained would improve gradually.

Much of this time I thought about the visit with the angels, wondering when they might appear again. There was an unmistakable feeling, like I had matured, that I had grown in understanding if not in spirit. I now possessed a vision of what follows life on Earth, and no one knew what I'd experienced. I wanted to tell someone, but thought it better not to, at least not then. It was a pleasant surprise that my recall of the angelic encounter was very clear and detailed. Evidently the mortar blast hadn't affected memory. Over and over I thought about all that happened since arriving in Nam, especially the discussion with Lawrence and James, and the visit from the Guardians.

The nurse from Philly and I became good friends during my three-day stay. On the second day she checked the registry and found that I was the only one in the hospital or the morgue from my unit. Afterward I called the first sergeant's office. His clerk said a few others received only minor injuries, and that I would get a Purple Heart.

The last day was spent with the nurse on her rounds. She had an orderly bring a new set of fatigues. It felt good to be up and doing something... and out of a hospital gown. But it was tragic seeing so many young men seriously injured. Many suffered terrible wounds, limbless, blind, deaf, burned, sometimes all four. I did my best to follow her example and keep a smile. It was a long day and this was her last shift in Nam. When the next shift arrived, she invited me to the USO for ice cream.

We sat and talked as we licked our cones, then went back for seconds. She had orders to process out the next day; to fly home and receive her discharge. Her wedding was set for the following week. She was happy. I didn't want to spoil her joy, but couldn't resist the opportunity to ask about her beliefs in an afterlife, having lived in a war zone for a year and seeing death nearly every day. When the right moment came, I said, "You think much about what's next? You've seen a lot of suffering and dying during your tour. Do you believe there's anything to look forward to after life here on Earth?"

"Funny you should ask," she said looking me in the eye. "I keep flashing on this one incident. About a month ago a young soldier arrived at the triage tent, mortally wounded. He had lost too much blood; a mine took off both legs and the medivac hadn't gotten there in time. We tried to save him, but it was hopeless. We didn't say so of course, but he knew he wasn't going to make it. I decided to stay with him, to hold his hand and listen to his last words. He was fully conscious and aware. I'll never forget the way he looked, and what he said just before dying. He saw something and spoke out loud and clear, 'Grammaw! Grampaw!!' Then he closed his eyes and died with the most peaceful smile on his face."

"Wow. What do you think he saw? You think he was hallucinating? Could it have been caused by morphine?" I asked.

"Don't know, but it was real to him. And just after he died, an old chaplain came by. I told him what happened. He said he'd seen this more than once, and that he believed these were visions of the next life, that the dying ones were being welcomed to the other side."

It felt like I could trust her, that she would not think me crazy, hearing about my meeting with the Guardians. My instinct was right; she listened and didn't judge. And we marveled over the fact that it was our grandparents who greeted her dying soldier and me. We talked for a little while longer, about her religious beliefs and the possibility of an afterlife. Then she was off to her going-home-party, to say good-bye to the team of nurses with whom she had worked for many months.

We stood and hugged. "You take care, Baker, ya hear?!" She kissed my cheek, then fished around in her pocket and handed over her thermometer as a souvenir. She said, "Good night, sleep well. I hope you see those angels again."

"And I hope you have a great wedding and a good life." We went our separate ways feeling the warmth and depth of friendship that war can bring.

Early next morning the doctor came by and pronounced me well enough to return to "light duty" for a week. I was dismissed and ordered to report to my unit. I went to the hospital's chopper pad and waited for a lift to Chu Lai. It wasn't a long wait. Two others, both with minor wounds, were aboard. On the way, I'll never forget, one of them referred to helicopters as "flying coffins."

The first sergeant assigned me to a small first-aid tent until recovery was complete. I worked alone treating minor problems—foot fungus, cuts and wounds, jungle infections and such. It was a chance to get to talk with a variety of men from many states and several countries. Australians, New Zealanders, Canadians, Philippinos, Thailanders, South Koreans, all were sent to Nam to fight alongside Americans.

During my recovery period, when there was no one needing treatment, I thought about the first five days in Nam. I was hoping there might be another meeting with the Guardians, at the same time wishing it wouldn't involve another injury. The details of my encounter with them were still very vivid. In fact, I could recall everything since arriving "in country" with crystal clarity. The angelic meeting played over and over in my mind, but I didn't mention it to anyone else.

After three days, I did begin to question why my angels hadn't been in contact. Then it hit me: I'd forgotten something crucial; that Joyah said to write down everything that happened. That evening I went to the PX and found a thick eight-by-six-inch journal with lined pages. When not treating cuts, scratches, and itches I wrote, then edited and reedited, until every detail was there and clearly stated. When ten or so pages were done I made legible copies on stationery and mailed them home. The week went by quickly, and soon enough, it was time to return to the field.

Chapter 5

LOVE

That last day in the rear, after gathering a new set of gear, I went over the journal notes one more time. It seemed kind of fantastic to read, certainly unlike life back home. Before lifting off that afternoon the first sergeant handed me a blue leather case with a Purple Heart medal inside. As I opened it he said, "See that you don't get another one, Baker." I couldn't help liking him; it was obvious he cared about his men.

Hot meals and cold canned drinks stored in three large insulated chests were loaded on the bird with me, along with two twenty-gallon plastic water bladders. The food smelled good. We landed on a hilltop where my platoon was camped. Lawrence and James ran over to help unload.

"Welcome back to the war," Lawrence yelled over the roar of the chopper. After it lifted off we carried the food and water to the lieutenant's tent.

James asked, "Did you get a Purple Heart, Ernie?" I dropped my ruck and pulled the medal out of a side pouch.

Just then Lieutenant Smithson walked up, not limping. "Glad you're OK, Baker. Not everybody gets a medal on their first day in the field. Don't let it happen again," he said with a slight smile.

"No, sir. I don't plan to."

He turned and yelled, "First squad, line up for chow." Lawrence, James, and I dished it out on flimsy paper plates. Each man got one soda and one beer. When all four squads and the lieutenant were fed, we filled our plates and sat on James and Lawrence's air mattresses.

"How was it lounging in the rear, Private Baker? You marry any handsome nurses while you were loafing?" Lawrence joked.

"Met a good one," I said. "We made friends. But she was headed home to her fiancé... What happened after I was knocked out? They said no one else was hurt, but I remember someone calling for a medic."

"The attack didn't last long," James answered. "Besides you there were a couple of little wounds. One guy was hit in the eye, from a flying rock. It wasn't that bad. He didn't medivac out with you. We wondered how bad you were hurt. That mortar landed right next to your hole. Lawrence and I weren't knocked out, but our ears rang for a while."

"The doc said I lost a little hearing. It got better after a few days. The first sergeant put me on light duty for a week. He had me patching cuts and treating feet. You guys see any more action?"

"While you were living easy back in the rear, we fought off three human wave attacks and captured an NVA regiment," Lawrence declared.

"Don't listen to him," James said with a chuckle. "It's been pretty peaceful. We went on one patrol after another without taking fire. Second and third platoons got into minor skirmishes on their patrols. One guy was hurt we heard. Just a few more days out here and we get a week in the rear. Good timing, Ern."

"We're staying here tonight?" I asked.

"Yep. Put up your tent and we'll start digging you a hole," Lawrence offered.

Just before sunset, another chopper landed leaving mail and taking away the empty food chests and water bladders. James shouted, "Mail's here." A cheer went up. He went around passing out letters and packages, then came back and handed me a fat letter. He gave Lawrence a copy of the *Stars and Stripes,* and then ripped open his own letter.

"I get a newspaper and you two get letters from home," Lawrence complained.

"Looks like a personal one Baker, I can smell the perfume from here." It was from Karen, scented with lilac, the first letter I'd received.

I opened it and showed the pictures she enclosed. "This is her with my mom and dad. That's our dog, Loopy, in front. And this is a picture of the painting she made of herself and me."

"What a cutie, Ern. And she's an artist! She's good. Looks just like you," James commented.

There was a letter from her and notes from both mom and dad. "She won an award, and has a show coming up at a local gallery. Mom says Loopy misses me. Dad said to wear my helmet, or else."

James reported on his letter, "My sister's getting married. Dang, wish I could be there, my family has great weddings... And my best friend Pete got a medical deferment. Bad eyesight. The army missed out on a great guitar player."

Lawrence said, "Well, you two home boys revel in your mail. I'm reading the really important news. Says here in the O-so-fficial Army News that some politicians are predicting the war will be over by Christmas. Everyone who believes that, stand up and salute."

"Which Christmas?" James asked cynically.

"Holy Hanoi, look at this, LBJ's quitting!" Lawrence held up the newspaper. "Listen up. He announced he wouldn't run, just last week. You know what this means, lads, Nixon will run against Kennedy."

"Maybe one of them will end this rotten war," James said wishfully. "Who are you voting for, Ern?"

"Don't know. Anyway, I'm too young to vote. Kind of strange, being old enough to go to war, but too young to vote."

"How old are you?" James asked.

"Twenty."

"You have a degree already?"

"I got through high school in three years, and college in three. A month later the draft board sent a mandatory invitation."

"That means you're too young to drink, too," Lawrence said. "Better give me your beer."

"Seriously guys, the voting laws are out of whack, aren't they? At least the law didn't stop me from taking CO status."

"That's right, Private Baker," Lawrence said. "You have the legal right to get killed without defending yourself, but not to vote or drink."

About then the sun was setting while the moon rose. The sky was a riot of colors that evening. Artillery fire could be heard in the far distance as insects began singing. Curious they weren't in the least aware of the war.

We sat there for a minute scanning the dry plain out to the horizon. I couldn't help wondering if there would be another mortar barrage in the night. And if my Guardians were present. It was too early to sleep. We decided to make hot chocolate. A packet with the mix of ingredients came in every box of rations.

As we sat there heating our cups, James said to Lawrence, "Speaking of the end of the war, Mr. Philosopher, tell us your thoughts on love and war, peace and fighting? Was philosophy your major? You went to college, didn't you?"

"I did two years at Arizona State, before Uncle Sugar beckoned me to this lovely little war party," Lawrence said, dipping a finger in his cup to see if it was hot. "Wasn't it a shame we were drafted just before the 'summer of love?' We spent most of '67 in training, preparing for war, not love. While we were in basic, our contemporaries were exploring newfound freedoms of body and mind in San Francisco. Free love... what a concept." He raised his cup and took a sip.

"We three probably agree on the gross insanity and utter baseness of war, having seen it first hand," Lawrence went on.

"Some fine day humans may cease solving their disagreements by shooting each other. We can only hope, pray, and wish for it. But love is a deeper subject. I suspect you're not asking about carnal love, brother James. It's interesting that the Greeks divide it into at least four categories: God's love, family affection, peer friendship, and sex passion. To which are you referring?"

James thought about it and asked, "Don't all those come from the same feeling?"

"James, James, you neglect your Scottish roots. Have you not read the wise Scotsman philosopher, John Duns Scotus, who put forth this thought jewel, 'If God is to be loved, then he is to be loved as God?' One must differentiate the levels of love. Can you say the love for a pet is on a par with the love for God? And isn't love more than a feeling?"

"Like most people, I ignored or neglected philosophy altogether, Mr. Encyclopedia," James replied a little indignantly. We laughed. "Anyway, what do you say love is, if it's not a feeling?"

Lawrence answered, "Isn't real love, soul-love, something selfless? There is a sort of love that seeks to possess, but that's a selfish love. No, my dear brothers-at-arms, genuine love craves to do good—not for self—but for others. True love isn't a feeling, rather a desire to share one's time and energy in ways that are mutually beneficial. In the end, real love benefits both the giver and the recipient. And a close examination of the matter indicates that love and goodness are closely related."

James and I were somewhat stunned at the depth of Lawrence's analysis and the breadth of his description of love. Again, I thought, 'What is a guy like him doing on a battlefield?' But it had become obvious that draft boards didn't care about a person's intellectual development or level of education, or even his potential value to society. An army needs warm bodies to carry out orders and carry weapons. In that regard, it didn't discriminate.

"Where have you seen that kind of goodness and love," I asked.

Lawrence replied, "A mother's love reaches that level, no?"

James said, "Both my parents love me and my sister that way. Unselfishly."

"Mine too, now that you mention it," I had to say. "So, why can't all humans treat each other with kindness and caring, not just our own families? Here we are in the middle of a killing zone talking about the highest reach of humans as we act out the lowest."

"Good point, brother Baker," Lawrence said. "There is an obvious and wide disconnect between familial affection and international fraternity. And history has shown that even within a nation, when we aren't fighting another country, we fight among ourselves. The US civil war saw over 600,000 deaths. And it behooves us to note the death toll is usually a small fraction of the injury count. Note also that no man, woman, or child who is exposed to war is left uninjured or unchanged. When our hitch is up, we won't be the same."

"I've already changed," James said. "I had to turn off a part of me that would normally care about somebody else. But another part of me can't forget those soldiers we kill with artillery, bombs, and bullets, they have families like I do; moms, dads, sisters, and brothers."

I had to ask, "Don't you hate it, hate turning off your heart?"

Lawrence quickly answered, "It's a soldier's duty, Objector Baker. Would you have us all lay down our weapons and capitulate to reason and compassion? What is wrong with you?!" We chuckled quietly.

"Not too late for you two to take objector status," I joked.

"Well now, what if everyone did that, especially if there's

a just war?" Lawrence asked. "We know that sometimes men have to defend their homes, their nations, even civilization itself."

"That's true. But do you think Vietnam is one of those times? If I thought this was a so-called 'just war,' I might have enlisted without taking objector status. But I'd still want to do something besides killing."

James said, "I never thought about a just war. Do you think Korea or World War II were just?"

Evidently the lieutenant, resting in his tent nearby, was overhearing us. He ordered, "Knock off the chatter and get some shut-eye you three." We followed his order and lay down quietly. I stared at the moon for a while thinking about the kinds of love Lawrence outlined, then rolled over and went to sleep.

During the night, Joyah and Rayah somehow appeared in my consciousness, very real like our first encounter. It was a delight to see their beaming faces once more. Meeting again also dissolved the faint doubt that had crept into my mind. We shared a warm embrace. There's nothing quite like an angelic hug I decided.

Rayah said enthusiastically, "We are very pleased you began a journal, and think you are wise to make a copy to send to your parents. We hope to make good use of your records when all is in readiness."

That made me curious. "What is your plan, exactly? What all can you or will you reveal? And when do you want it to be published?"

"Let us leave the question of publication open for now. There are many things to reveal," Joyah answered. "The discussion with your fellows this evening makes for an excellent starting point."

"You're aware of everything I do, everything I see and hear, aren't you?"

Rayah answered with charm and undeniable affection.

"Ernie, you may be sure we are cognizant of all that goes on within your realm of consciousness. One or both of us is always in attendance upon you. You are our sole assignment and our primary responsibility. We are your Guardians but also your friends and kindred spirits. We love you with an angelic affection."

I was so touched by her sincerity that I reached out for their hands and looked them in the eyes. There was such beauty of honesty and fearless affection in them that all my social inhibitions were forgotten. "If only every human could know the angels," I thought. I felt a curious urge to both laugh and cry for joy.

Joyah smiled, and then said, "Your friend Lawrence spoke well of love, a good primer for what Rayah and I wish to convey on the subject. We would begin by bringing forth the irrefutable fact that love must have a source."

Rayah added, "Sooner or later, all ascending beings come to recognize that love has a source. That recognition is followed by an irresistible desire to know that source. And it should be noted in this connection, that love can exist only between persons. Humans all too often say they love this or that thing, but in fact, true love, genuine love, can only be realized in the relationships and interactions between personal beings."

Joyah went on, "Love, Ernie, is actually the most compelling of all influences in the cosmos. Remember this: In spite of any and all evidence to the contrary, genuine love is the most real of all experiences between persons. Nothing outranks or supersedes it. Nothing."

"And its source?" I very much wanted to hear their answer.

Rayah replied, "If you realize that love is a reaction to being loved, you will have to acknowledge that there had to be someone, somewhere, who was the first to love. And that realization should bring you face to face with love's source. Ever remember that all love is a response to love previously bestowed."

It then dawned on me where they were going, what they were attempting to teach. "The source has to be God, doesn't it?"

Joyah answered, "Your friend Lawrence was correct to say there is a First Person of the universe, the creator of all subsequent personalities and spirit beings. And we can tell you that this First Person is one and the same as the being you refer to as God. God is the word humans apply to the one we know as the Universal Father. And we would further inform you that the Universal Father's primary and overarching attitude is one of love. Our Heavenly Father is indeed the original source and the final destiny of love. God the Creator first loved us so that in turn, and in time, we will willingly and joyously return that love to its source. This is accomplished in selfless service, treating others as you wish to be treated. The circle of love is from the Father of Love to you and back to God. Love cannot be realized unless and until it is shared."

Rayah added, "Lawrence was also correct in saying you have, at your core, as your essence, a fragment of God, living within. There resides within you, the living presence of our loving Father. Eventually you, and every human who truly wishes it, will discover this indwelling presence of divine love. This discovery will come through the gateway of mind, and by no other means than love, for God must be loved to be known. We can say with absolute assurance that the one you call God wants you to know of the divine presence living within. And that presence is none other than the source of love, a magnificent and adoring being of transcendent grace and unlimited goodness. One who asks only that you believe in love, and by your selfless acts, return this love to its source, thereby completing the circle of divine affection surrounding Creator and creature and touching all within. For love is contagious."

This is the last thing they imparted that night, something

I've never forgotten, since Joyah stated it so emphatically: "We must emphasize that humans have a choice. They can choose to accept or reject the love of God. But you must also know that God wants all his children to accept his love. It is the divine desire that all humanity receive even the gift of eternal life. No one can be forced to live forever, but you must have that choice if there is to be free will. Rejection of divine love is always a possibility when Creators bestow free will upon their creatures."

Rayah said, "Let this be enough for now. You have quite a bit to recall and record. Thank you, Ernie, we deeply appreciate your willingness to hear us and to help us with our assignment."

I wanted to go on, but knew they were right to end it there. We hugged and the next thing I recall was opening my eyes and seeing the moon setting on the western horizon. Heavy dew had come in the night. I lay awake thinking about and reviewing the discussion with my Guardians, and with Lawrence and James before that. I was up before daybreak writing everything down, from both conversations.

Chapter 6

TORTURE

After daybreak the lieutenant was up and summoning the squad leaders. He ordered the platoon to have breakfast, pack up, and be ready to move out at 0700. Lawrence, James, and I opened canned C-rations of meat, cheese, jelly and crackers. We mixed instant coffee with sugar, powdered cream, and water, then heated it. Hardly a word was said. My mind was busy going over the morning's journal notes. After breakfast, I added a few lines that popped into my head while we were waiting for the order to leave.

There was enough time left to brush my teeth, and to put a fresh bandage on the lieutenant's toe. It was healing nicely and wasn't infected. I complimented him on taking good care of it in my absence. While I wrapped it, he said to Lawrence and James, "We're meeting with a two-man recon team at this village." He pointed to a spot on his map and said we would move out in five minutes. I later learned reconnaissance agents secretly moved around the countryside alone or in small groups gathering information and feeding it to the commanders in the rear.

It was already hot when we descended the hill. We walked several kilometers across dry rice paddies. On one of our breaks, James told me that farmers already harvested their rice crops and had to wait for the next monsoon season to plant, around October.

Even before arriving at the edge of the village, we could hear men speaking loudly in Vietnamese. As we got closer, I saw two Americans in crisp, clean fatigues manhandling a small shirtless Vietnamese in black silk pants. His hands were tied behind his back. It was obvious the two men were questioning him, and he was vigorously denying everything. All three of them were yelling back and forth. The two Americans then forced the man's head into a barrel of water and held him there as he wriggled and gurgled. He was allowed up for a quick breath. And after another plunge, they yanked him up and screamed more questions at him. He gasped, coughed, sputtered, and presumably, denied knowing anything. They stuck his head under water again, holding him down what seemed like a long time. We watched in astonished horror. Smithson didn't say or do anything.

"Those guys are outfitted as Special Forces but they're probably CIA, working out here in the boonies," James told me in low voice.

A righteous indignation began swelling in my craw as they repeatedly dunked this skinny and progressively exhausted man. I went to the lieutenant and said forcefully, "Sir, isn't torture illegal according to the Geneva Convention?"

All he said was, "At ease, Private." I wasn't at ease at all. And the longer this went on, the angrier I got.

"Sir, this is not right!" I yelled out after another dunking. The two interrogators heard it. When they looked at me, I said in a loud voice, "This is NOT legal!"

The lieutenant approached and spoke quietly with the interrogators as their captive coughed and breathed heavily, slumping to the ground next to the barrel. One of them glared at me as Smithson talked and then said something into his walkie-talkie. They ceased tormenting the man and moved him to a nearby clearing. A few minutes later a helicopter arrived. All three boarded and took off. That was the last we saw of them. The lieutenant gave me a sideways glance but didn't say anything except, "Move out."

The platoon cautiously walked into the village and began searching each hut for weapons, explosives, and tunnels. Women and children in each hut huddled fearfully, clutching each other. The mothers spoke out in Vietnamese, undoubtedly proclaiming innocence and protesting the home invasion. It was notable that no young men or boys were present. Lawrence,

James, and I took a position with the lieutenant at the center of the village while the squads searched every structure. It was high noon by the time the search was done and we all relaxed a bit.

"Take a lunch break in place," Smithson ordered the squad leaders over the radio. "Be ready to move out at 1300." We four took rations from our rucks and ate out of the cans. No one had much appetite.

Nothing was said for a long while, so finally I asked, "Sir, are you going to report what we saw?"

He shot back, "Are you?"

"Not if you do," I replied.

"I'll put it in my daily report, Baker. Let it be."

Lawrence and James didn't say a word, but we knew his daily report would most likely go unread, or unnoticed. The lieutenant quickly finished his rations and left to confer with the squad leaders about their findings and the platoon's next move.

"Am I the only one who thought that was torture?"

James answered, "No, and I'm glad you said something."

Lawrence said, "It was torture, and illegal. The second causality of war is legality, after truth. Them that run the war don't respect conventions. Look no farther than Agent Orange being sprayed on the jungles west of here. Chemical warfare was outlawed after WWI, but we do it anyway."

"Why aren't you infuriated, why isn't everyone infuriated? Dammit!"

"Nature of the beast," Lawrence quipped.

James looked at me with sad eyes, saying nothing. I grabbed the med-pouch and went looking for someone to treat. One of the villagers let me disinfect and bandage her daughter's injured arm. Evidently an animal had bitten her.

At the appointed time we moved out, making our way west. Most of the afternoon we tramped across barren paddies, taking breaks once an hour or so, until reaching the edge of the jungle. Then we slowly hacked our way through dense brush up a foothill that was to be our overnight camp. After everyone dug their foxhole, set up tents and hammocks, and had a bite to eat, Smithson coordinated night watch. He then retired to his tent scribbling out a daily report. Lawrence, James, and I were plenty tired but not ready to bed down. We made hot chocolate and watched the moon rise. While the canteen cups heated we applied mosquito repellant.

As we sat there in a state of near exhaustion, James asked Lawrence, "Do you know exactly what the Geneva Convention says about dunking people to get info, and about spraying the jungle?"

Lawrence thought a minute before answering, "As I recall, it defines torture as inflicting pain or suffering. You would think that's clear and indisputable, but the military might not call what we saw today torture. Besides, who's enforcing it? And I remember reading, probably a couple of years ago, when congress found out about the use of herbicides, they were assured these agents aren't chemical weapons. The military claimed it killed only the crops that were feeding the enemy. But some experts say those herbicides can cause cancer and deformities in offspring."

I felt anger again, at having to participate in such a war. I wondered aloud, "What do you think we're really doing in Vietnam?"

"Ostensibly, stopping Chinese communism from spreading to all East Asia," Lawrence replied.

"You think we can?" James asked.

"Doesn't look like it now, after Tet," said Lawrence. "It appears as though America will go the way of the French before us, retreating home in defeat."

"I don't understand how people can treat each other the way we do. Even animals aren't that cruel," I lamented. "It has to weigh on their souls. When the war is over, how will those who torture and cause famines live with themselves?"

"Some won't live. The suicide rate for combat veterans is high. And those who torture are often tortured by their past," Lawrence said with some sadness.

James opined, "This is depressing. Just last night we talked about what love is. Now we talk about ugly suffering, and we can't blame anyone except ourselves. You don't think God likes war, do you?"

Lawrence replied, "Nationalism and war are fairly prevalent in some of the world's most popular scriptures, but the question is, do they truly represent God's wishes, God's commandments?"

"If God is love, then no." James answered.

"Who can say with absolute authority what God's attitude is?" Lawrence asked pointedly. I immediately reflected on the Guardians' words about God being the source and destiny of love.

I said, "If God is good—and the religions I know about teach that God is good—even the standard of goodness, then how can a religion's followers do such mean things to others? Treat one another worse than animals treat each other?"

"People's standards can all too easily fall into the dirt, Objector Ernie," Lawrence said looking up at the rising moon and lying back on his air mattress. James and I lay down too. We were bone-tired.

"If God really is good, then why is there so much suffering in the world," James asked.

"You asked that question before, Thanes-man," Lawrence replied. "But we veered onto a discussion of providence, as I recall."

"So, how do you philosophers answer questions about the reason for suffering?" I asked.

After a moment's hesitation, Lawrence said, "There's more than one school of thought. But there is general agreement that humans bring most suffering on themselves, by poor planning and shortsightedness, by impatience and intolerance. Sure, there are floods, earthquakes, and diseases, natural causes of suffering. But then one has to acknowledge the fact that we humans choose to build our houses on lowlands known to be flood-zones. We erect skyscrapers on top of soft ground and over fault-lines. We construct our edifices out of flammable materials. We even get careless about what's in our drinking water. The majority of diseases are caused by bad habits, poor nutrition, even self-abuse. Consider also the fact that humans, not God, let hatred grow in our minds and hearts. Most often because of skin tone, governmental ideology, or differing religious beliefs. For all our powers of innovation and cleverness, we don't act that smart."

"And are philosophers immune from all those human flaws?" James asked wryly.

"Oh, we are," Lawrence replied. "Paragons of learning, wisdom and virtue, all! I'm up for sainthood, didn't I mention it?" That brought a laugh that felt good.

"Knock off the noise!" the lieutenant barked out. "Hit the hay, chatter-heads." But I suspected he liked overhearing our discussions.

Chapter 7

FREE WILL

Sometime in the night I woke up in a sweat, after dreaming about the torture incident. In the dream, it was me being repeatedly dunked. I lay there awhile trying to shake off the terror, at the same time feeling relief it was only a dream. After a while sleep returned.

The next thing I remember is being back in the presence of the Guardians. It felt so good, so safe and friendly. What a contrast to the environment of war! We three embraced. Once again it made me want to weep and laugh with joy. Then it dawned on me that they had surely witnessed the torture episode.

"I forget that one or both of you are with me all the time. Maybe I'll get used to you being near... I'm wondering what you think when you see what happened yesterday, seeing that man being interrogated."

Joyah said, "Like you, it is difficult for us to observe such cruel treatment."

"Why do you think life has such cruelty, and so many wars? You told me about God's love last night, how the universe is filled with it. So why doesn't it show more on Earth? 'As above, so below,' isn't really true, is it?"

Rayah answered saying, "Someday selfless love will rule the hearts and minds of mortals, but your world must evolve. God cannot, or at least does not, intervene in the gradual progress of humanity. Social and civil evolution may seem slow to short-lived mortals, but it is very effective over time. And every step forward in the growth of universal love must be earned. The hand of Providence does not interfere in the natural, gradual unfolding of planetary life. But you should never doubt that the arc of progress is toward goodness. Love will prevail in the end. Righteousness, kindness, and virtue will triumph over evil, hate, and wrongdoing. History shows that humanity has evolved from savage tribalism to the organized civilization of today. It takes ages for people to realize that interest in the welfare of others actually enhances self-interest. Humans will eventually come to see that the desire to do good to others is also good for self. Be patient, and at the same time, work for the uplift of your fellows. Progress is in motion, but it is hardly finished, or perfect, on Earth."

Joyah added, "Ernie, we would instruct you in the long-view. We would ask that you attempt to see all things and events from the grand perspective, from God's point of view. God, with perfect and divine wisdom, does not intervene every time a creature transgresses the boundaries of goodness. The Father of Love may be trusted always to do what is the greatest good for the greatest number. You should attempt to do this as well. Mortals are granted a certain range of free will, and this is always respected, at least we have never seen it overruled in some arbitrary act of divine intervention. Great suffering may come from human ignorance and cruelty, but in the end all things and beings must bend to the arc of goodness. Those who will not bend, break. By their stubbornness and willful disregard for the welfare of others, some will forgo goodness. They will, thereby, run the risk of losing the opportunity to serve the greater good in time and eternity."

"So, some will not survive into the afterlife? Are you telling me they end up in hell?"

"Ernie, there is no hell except the one mortals create," Rayah said firmly. "You may recall reading in scripture, 'the wages of sin is death.' There is no punishment except the self-chosen cessation of existence. God, who is motivated by divine love, is not wrathful and doesn't punish his erring offspring. Every normal-minded human may exercise their own free will choice for choosing either good or evil. Choosing evil has inevitable consequences, just as does choosing good. But even if evil is chosen, there is allowance; there is a great buffer zone of understanding mercy. Given free will, humans will invariably choose unwisely and make mistakes. This is an inevitable feature that is woven into life. Unwise choosing, making mistakes, generates consequences—even opportunities—to reevaluate and correct. Wisdom and character are forged by your choices, both wise and unwise. Divine mercy affords a time delay in which the wrongdoer may correct course, and choose more wisely in the future. When you think of God's mercy, think of a parent's attitude toward his or her beloved child."

"I never could believe there is a hell. I always felt like the universe is good even if people weren't. And I couldn't help wondering what kind of God would burn people forever. But I never thought much about mercy."

"Think about this," Joyah replied. "If mortal life is designed so that lessons are learned from making decisions—if there truly is free will—then you must have the freedom of making poor choices. The Father of Love knows the creature's natural situation, knows that you learn best from mistakes and failures. Ernie, mistakes and conflict are necessary parts of life. One must choose between good and evil in order to discover and adopt spiritual values. It is such values that shapes character. No one passes through life without conflict, error, and failure. These very conflicts, errors, and failures determine and promote survival character. Character, embraced spiritual value, is the substance of the soul. And wise men know that character is measured, not by the number of accomplishments or failures, but by intent. The Creator, who indwells you, looks into your heart. Your intentions reveal the core of your character, not your mistakes or achievements. The grace of mercy means that whatever is not achieved during life in the flesh, will be in time—IF it is worthy, if it has genuine spiritual value, soul-meaning."

"So, you're saying suffering is necessary? I have a hard time believing all life's harshness has purpose and value. What was the point of that man's water torture?"

"You may be certain that the God of Universal Love who indwells every human heart is tormented on being forced to endure such reprehensible human acts. Indeed, the torment is doubled since God indwells both the victim and the perpetrator. Your friend Lawrence was correct in saying that most human suffering is self-created. People abuse their God-given free will in sometimes-atrocious ways. Humans all too often ignore obvious hazards; they often leap without looking. Important decisions demand reflective thinking. Humans can be hasty, impatient, and self-centered, and thereby suffer unfortunate consequences by their own acts. Some of those consequences reverberate down the generations. They can and do manifest as war, racial hatred, and unfeeling cruelty," said Rayah.

"Must be frustrating for you angels."

"We understand how you might think that," Joyah replied. "But we have the advantage of the long view, which fosters a tolerant understanding of your errors. Humans cannot be expected to know all there is to know during one brief life. Mistakes, some of which lead to devastating outcomes, are common. Hear us when we say that life on Earth is short, that you will, after survival, be able to build on the foundation of spiritual values that you embraced during your brief sojourn in the flesh. It is but a beginning, this life as a human. You can hardly imagine a life after this that is much longer, even eternal. But we gave you a glimpse of the next life in seeing your resurrected grandparents. Beyond that life lies untold ages of progress in spirit and advancement in status, until that day when you meet God in person, at the center of all things and beings, on the Isle of Paradise."

That made me fire off several questions. "How long have you been alive? Have you met God, face-to-face?"

Rayah responded, "We were created over two hundred thousand Earth years ago. Since then we have served in a variety of ways. Our order of angels—and there are many orders—are known as Seraphim. A primary seraphic responsibility is the watch-care, the spiritual oversight, of humans like you. We undergo extensive training before assuming our duties. We are trained to minister to the spiritual needs of all kinds of creatures, most of whom are like humans.

53

Over long periods of instruction and hands-on training, we have become masters of thousands of languages and developed diverse skills associated with various kinds of ministries. Angelic existence transcends your human life because we were created slightly higher than you, and we do not age. But we have similarities to you. We too are designed to ascend, to someday meet the Universal Father on Paradise. We progress through increasing service to others, especially humans. We will go with you and remain at your side throughout your career as an ascending mortal. Before being attached to you we served together on many missions of group ministry, but you are our first assignment as personal Guardians. If you survive, if you do not reject eternal life, we will be your friends and Guardians for a very long time, as you regard time. We already have eternity status; now it brings us joy and satisfaction to guide a human into spiritual maturity and unending life."

It was time to ask the question each of us ponders in our heart: "Will I survive?"

"It is wholly your choice, Ernie. But the acceptance of this unusual mission bodes well for your eternal prospects," Joyah replied. "The option to serve only one's self and reject life is always open, even after you resurrect at the level where your grandparents are now. But we know you have what is required for survival, which is faith. In your short life, already have you shown many qualities of enduring spiritual value, more so than most of your fellows. The possession of true moral character, genuine spirituality, was evident in your reactions to the man being subjected to cruel interrogation. And before that in choosing not to kill. You displayed a God-like compassion when you chose a career as a healer, a caretaker of your fellows, and a non-combatant. Even before that, as a child, you showed a remarkable capacity for empathy and understanding."

I then inquired, "What do you mean by reject life? Is suicide rejection? I've thought about that and wondered what happens to people who kill themselves."

"The taking of one's own life should be viewed from a mercy perspective," Rayah answered. "Never forget, intention is everything to God, and humans do not have that superhuman insight to be able to discern intention accurately. Lawrence mentioned your fellow soldier suicides; some of them take their lives in order to avoid doing harm to others. All too often, men and women have endured the terrible trials of war. Many of them will have to deal with feelings of homicidal anger and self-hatred well after the war. Rather than take out that anger and hate on their enemies, some will turn it on themselves... Even more tragic, they often turn it on their loved ones, too.

"Consider also the suicide of one who is terminally ill. These individuals know their family is suffering with them, and do not wish to prolong the emotional trauma. Other suicide cases are related to mental and physical disorders, the inability to be happy, to enjoy life. Such individuals may suffer many decades before ending life by their own hand. But there is no excuse for wasting life, giving up for no reason. The lessons of life in the flesh are important and not to be simply dismissed because they are challenging. In every case our Heavenly Father knows the person's intention. Life cannot be forced on anyone, but we know that our loving God wishes that none should perish in time or eternity. Remember always, when you think of God's attitude toward his creatures, think of the ideal attitude of a wise and loving parent for a child. That should answer most of your questions regarding survival and intention."

Joyah said, "You have much to think over, and much to record, Ernie. Go back to your rest. And forget not our constant presence."

I woke just before daybreak. I thought about what was to go in the journal, from the conversation with Lawrence and James, as well as my Guardians. When there was enough light, I wrote it down. Memory of all that was said seemed to flow easily. I wondered if maybe the Guardians were prompting me somehow.

55

Chapter 8

BACKTRACK

Just as the sun peeked above the horizon a message came over the radio, "Alpha Charlie One, do you read?"

James sat up and grabbed the mic, "Alpha Charlie One, good morning Delta base."

"New orders. Put your Charlie Oscar on." James took the radio to the lieutenant. He scribbled as he listened then signed off. He decoded the coordinates he was given and looked at his map.

"Get the squad leaders, we're going back. Get ready to move out at..." he looked at his watch, "0730 hours."

James switched the channel on his radio and conveyed the lieutenant's move-out time to the squad leaders.

"Back where, Sir?" James asked.

"To that village," Smithson replied with exasperation at apparent army confusion.

James had a puzzled look. "Why, Sir? There was nothing there."

"Ours is not to ask why, Corporal. Be ready to move out at 0730."

We broke out rations, heated coffee, had breakfast, then packed our rucks, still wondering why we had to backtrack all that way to a village that didn't appear to have military value or enemy presence.

Descending the hill was as slow and difficult as ascending it. The lieutenant didn't want to take the path we hacked out going up, fearing that route might have been booby trapped while we slept. We then marched across the plain in sweltering heat and humidity. There was hardly a breeze. We were drenched in sweat before long. During the first break, I advised the newest men in the field to drink lots of water and take a salt tablet.

It was just before noon, not far from the village, that we heard over the radio the other three platoons were closing in. Just then we received AK47 fire. Bullets zinged overhead.

"Take cover!" Smithson shouted. We all went down behind the nearest dike. "Get Captain Stone on the horn, Corporal." James complied then handed the mic to the lieutenant. There was an exchange of words about joining all four platoons to form an unbroken perimeter around the village. After that Smithson switched the radio frequency and relayed the captain's order to our four squads. A firefight broke out on the opposite side of the village. We fanned out, keeping low, and connected with the two platoons on our flanks. The lieutenant, Lawrence, James, and I were in the approximate center of our platoon's portion of the perimeter.

Just after we took positions behind dikes and dropped our rucks, more shots were fired at us, many more. They had AK's and machine guns. The fire was coming from bamboo hedges all around the village's outskirts. Everyone stayed low and returned fire.

"We must have missed something yesterday," James yelled between short bursts that he and Lawrence were firing.

Smithson sent out another radio message to the squads, "Hold your position and conserve your ammo." Then to Lawrence, "Get some 155's on that hedgerow." Lawrence checked his map and gave the coordinates to James who radioed them to the artillery battery in the rear. A minute later a smoke round landed in front of our position. Lawrence took the mic and called in a correction. The next round landed right on the hedgerow. But that didn't stop the machine gun fire.

"There must be a nest of them, well dug in," the lieutenant said. Then we heard jets approaching. Evidently, Captain Stone called for air support. The first napalm missed the hedgerows and hit inside the village, spreading orange fire and smoke across a wide area. More jets followed dropping bombs and napalm. We could hear AK and machine gun fire going out from positions that surrounded the village. More artillery and bombs were called in. But the bullets kept coming from the hedges.

"They're dug in good," Smithson said. "Look! They aren't VC. It's NVA!" He pointed to three men in North Vietnamese dress running away from a fire set by the napalm. He radioed the company commander who then called for more jet sorties.

Over the next two hours a tremendous number of bombs, both explosive and napalm, plus artillery, were dropped around and in the village. One mortar round came our way, but no one was hit. Then the bullets gradually stopped flying overhead as the bombs and artillery found their targets.

It was blistering hot lying there in the midday sun. Occasionally a cloud would bring relief. Finally, after a few minutes without receiving fire, the order came to "approach and clear" the village. We put on our rucks and began walking slowly toward the burned-out village.

Before we got to the hedgerow, wherefrom much enemy fire had come, a woman followed by two children ran toward us. She was screaming something in Vietnamese. It was obvious to me they weren't a threat. They were burned, and their clothes, what was left of them, was in tatters and shreds. A man in first squad fired at her with several rounds. She fell. The children stopped and knelt at her side, wailing.

"Cease fire!" the lieutenant yelled out. I ran to the woman. Bullets had hit her in the chest and arm. With her last breath, she said something to the children. They collapsed at her side sobbing and looking at us, fearing they would be shot too.

Smithson looked down on us somewhat anguished and said, "Let's move out."

"Sir, what about the kids?" I asked.

He shouted out, "First squad! Take charge of the children

and any other non-combatants we find." The first squad leader assigned four men who surrounded the children and their dead mother.

"Watch for mines and traps, men," said Smithson as he and the others resumed approaching the now bombed-out enemy positions. I stayed with the children, until an AK47 shot came out of the hedgerow and hit a man in the fourth squad. Everyone went to the ground. A wounded and crazed NVA soldier stuck his head up and tried to fire again. Before he could, a hail of bullets felled him.

"Medic!" I ran to our wounded man. A bullet had passed through his right lung. He was panting hard, trying to catch his breath. There were sucking sounds coming from where the bullet had entered and exited.

"James, medivac!" I shouted, and then dug in the med-pouch for large bandages to cover both holes. As soon as they were covered he stopped panting. But I knew blood would soon fill that lung. He needed hospital help and soon.

"Am I going to die?" he asked. He was remarkably calm in spite of obvious pain and trauma.

"No, just take it easy, a chopper is on the way. I'm giving you a shot of morphine. You'll be OK. This could be your ticket home. And you'll get a Purple Heart." I hoped that was the right thing to say. I looked at his nametag and asked, "Connors, what's your first name?"

"Malcolm. If I don't make it, will you write my wife? Tell her I love her." He had an agonizing cough then whispered, "Her picture and address are in my wallet." He put his hand on his left shirt pocket. I pulled it out and found her picture with an address on the back. Just then I heard the medivac approaching. I put the wallet back. One of the men guarding the children threw me a smoke grenade. I pulled the pin and tossed it a few feet away. Yellow smoke went up and a chopper with big red crosses landed there. A medic jumped off and helped me load Malcolm.

As we put him on board, he grabbed my lapels and mouthed the words, "Please write her." His calmness was giving way to fear and shock.

"I won't have to, you're going to make it," I yelled over the rotor noise. "Take good care of him," I said to the medic on board. She nodded her head and began examining his wound. Just then two more wounded men, from the other platoons, were brought and loaded onto the bird. One was badly hurt and unconscious. The other had a leg wound. As the chopper lifted off the medic looked down and gave me a thumbs-up. Malcolm was trying to hand her his wallet.

The platoon was cautiously searching the smoldering hedgerow for other enemy survivors and casualties. On the way to rejoin them I passed by the two weeping children still at the dead woman's side. They looked up at me. A tear came to my eye as I wondered how many more women and children were in the village. Mournful cries were coming from inside, but no more rifle fire. There were many dead NVA soldiers. If there were a hell, this would be a scene in it.

In the village, only a few huts were left standing, and they were damaged. Inside the huts were those who somehow escaped the bombing, burning, and bullets. All were sobbing and fearful. They were herded to a central location in the open; only fifteen were found. The two children whose mother was shot were brought in. All were traumatized, wounded, or burned. As they wept and whimpered I treated as many as possible with what I had and asked the lieutenant to call in medivacs to transport them to the hospital.

He didn't respond, except to say, "Do what you can." He then ordered that the remaining structures of the village be burned. I stopped bandaging and went to him.

"Sir, we're not going to help these survivors? And we are going to burn down what's left of their homes?"

"Orders, Baker. This is an NVA village."

"Sir, we don't know that. The NVA could have taken over the village after we left yesterday. You know we didn't find anything here."

"At ease, Baker. Tend to your job."

I felt a rage take over, and began yelling at him. "What is wrong with you?! Are you dead inside? These people need help. Are we going to just walk away from here and leave them to suffer and die?"

He stared at me with cold eyes and said loudly, "We have our orders, Private, now get back to your duties." He turned to everyone who was watching and ordered them, "Destroy those hooches!" They all slowly turned away and began setting fire to the thatched roofs.

I went back to bandaging and comforting as best I could. The whole company searched the rubble and counted bodies. Three NVA were found still alive, but badly wounded. Before long they were loaded onto choppers and taken away, presumably for interrogation.

The company spent the rest of the day in and around the village, counting the dead soldiers and their weapons. I stayed with the village survivors, treating their injuries, until we were ordered to move out. When I heard that I became livid. We couldn't just leave the villagers, all children and old women, behind.

I protested again, this time to the company commander, Captain Stone. "Sir, we can't leave the survivors. These people are injured, homeless, and without water or food."

He looked at me, somewhat perplexed, then said to his radioman, "Sergeant, get two birds in here and evacuate these civilians."

"Yes, sir," he replied. "Where to, sir?"

"Da Nang hospital."

The other three platoons of the company were ordered to

move out and bivouac overnight in the rice paddies not far from the village. Our platoon stayed behind waiting for the evacuation choppers. It wasn't long before they arrived. Survivors were taken away, after which we marched off to rejoin the company. Not much was said all that time. Just about everyone was sick with residual gloom and death trauma.

Chapter 9

AFTERMATH

It was almost sunset when our platoon arrived at the bivouac site. We quickly dug shallow foxholes then heated our rations but didn't bother putting up tents. James, Lawrence and I were away from the lieutenant on this night. He camped with the company commander's group at the perimeter's center.

While the rations heated, we blew up our air mattresses and sat down to have a meal. The evening twilight was beautiful, and it was somewhat cooler. After a few bites the man who shot the woman approached and sat down, his head hanging low. He began to sob. He had dark red hair and a tattoo on his right forearm. The tattoo was of a large purple, vine-covered heart, with "Mom" underneath.

I looked at his nametag and asked, "You OK, Mason?" He wiped his eyes. Lawrence and James stopped eating but didn't say anything.

He choked out the words, "I shouldn't have shot her. But I was scared, and she was coming right at us." He paused, his chin atremble. He tried to find his voice again. "I thought she might have a grenade in her hand. But I didn't take time to check for sure."

We sat there silent. He couldn't control his tears. After a minute he said, "I keep seeing the faces of those crying kids, kneeling by her body."

I searched my mind for something to say or do. James and Lawrence were equally perplexed. After a minute I asked, "What's your name?"

"Ralph," he croaked.

James cleared his throat and said sympathetically, "Ralph, you didn't know if she had a grenade. Our training taught

63

us not to trust anyone, even kids. If she had a grenade, you might have saved several of our guys."

"But I didn't wait to see, I was scared!" he blubbered loudly and coughed. "And now those little kids hate me. And I hate me." He collapsed to the ground sobbing. This heartfelt anguish and grief caught the attention of everyone within earshot.

Ralph's squad leader came and put a hand on his shoulder. "Skip guard duty tonight, Mason," he said. "Get some rest."

I quickly dug two sedative tablets out of the med-pouch and told him to take them. He stood and stumbled away with the squad leader, sniffling and trying to contain himself.

Nothing was said for a while. Finally, James broke the silence, "You know, I don't think the lieutenant likes what we do any more than you, Ernie. But he was trained to follow orders, do what he is told no matter what. You've put him on the spot twice already. To tell you the truth, I'm glad you did, both times. But you may have to pay for it."

"I know. I've tried before to hold my tongue. I just can't keep my mouth shut when people are suffering, when something is unfair. It's a personal failing."

"If it is a failing, it's a benign one," Lawrence said. "But speaking out will get you into beaucoup hot water in this insane war, where morality and fairness are upside down. That said, I do admire your willingness to stand up, notwithstanding the probability that you won't last long out here. I, for one, will miss you."

James added, "He's right. Questioning orders is a no-no. I was amazed that the captain didn't dress you down when you said what you did. He must have felt something for those poor villagers. For all we know they didn't have anything to do with the NVA showing up and taking over. There was no sign of sympathy with the enemy when we searched their village yesterday."

"Maybe Captain Stone was right. He told me I didn't belong here on the first day. And I figured being a hotheaded Conscientious Objector would get me into trouble. Some of my relatives were CO's in World War I. They were Seventh Day Adventists. The government had them serve in hospitals. Or made them ambulance drivers and medics in the field. I guess CO's in the US are the lucky ones. Some countries send us to prison. My cousin said Hitler executed all CO's."

"Jehovah Witnesses are famed for their refusal to serve in war in any capacity, even dying for their beliefs," Lawrence said. "And the Catholics declared one of their German acolytes a martyr after he was executed for refusing to pick up a weapon and fight for Nazism during WW II. They even beatified him. You have a patron saint, Private Baker."

"I'm Catholic. What was his name?" James asked.

"Jaggerstatter," Lawrence replied. "Fritz. No Franz, I think."

There wasn't much energy for long conversations or hot chocolate. It was late and all were tired. We put on mosquito repellant and slept under the moon and stars. I went to sleep thinking about poor Ralph, but then had a dream about Karen. She was painting angels. She wanted them to appear as beings of light, but without wings and feathers. I told her how much they resembled Rayah and Joyah.

Sometime later in the night my Guardians paid a visit. It was good to see their beaming faces and their warm smiles once again. If they are a reflection of God, then God is truly good and bursting with friendliness. I reached out and took them, one in each arm. Their embrace exuded such love and unbounded affection that I had an urge to say, "Thank you." They seemed to understand why I thanked them. At that moment, I was struck once more by the profound difference between the heartless war of the day, and the affectionate angelic visits of the night.

65

Then it occurred to me that Joyah and Rayah might know the background and survival status of the mother Ralph Mason killed. "What do you know about that woman, the one who died in the battle yesterday? Where is she now? Did she survive? What actually happens when someone leaves their body permanently? You told me about living on in eternity last time. Did she wake up in another body? Where exactly do people go when they die? You gave some answers at our first meeting. And I remember Nana and Grandad talked about where they are, about getting a new, young body. You mentioned resurrection, how does that happen? Can you, or will you, tell me more about her fate?"

Joyah answered, "So many questions, Ernie, and good ones. The woman who perished was the mother of ten. Eight of her oldest children enlisted in the army of South Vietnam, as did her husband. He and the eight children lost their lives to a landmine while traveling home for a holiday visit two years ago. The two youngest were still at home. They were the ones you saw at her side when she died. She is a woman of extraordinary character and strength. She will be resurrected in new form on the first mansion world on the third day after her death."

Joyah went on, saying, "You may recall a reference to the mansion worlds and resurrection in a scriptural verse. It states, 'In my Father's house there are many mansions.' In fact, there are seven of these mansion worlds. They are but the first of many worlds to which mortals ascend during the initial stages of the eternal career. You were informed that your grandparents are now in residence on Mansion One, after having been resurrected in new form. The body you will have there is different from the one you have now. It is made of a substance unknown to you. It might be described as semi-material when compared to the human body. Our forms are something like the new body you will obtain on the occasion of your awakening in Resurrection Hall. That is where the mortal soul is reunited with the fragment of God that indwelt you during life in the flesh. Resurrection Hall is where you begin everlasting life."

Rayah said, "Ernie, we plan to reveal more about the mansion worlds and your next life in the first heaven. But now we would return you to your rest."

She spoke with such genuine charm and grace. I couldn't help feeling love for these Guardians. It wasn't my custom, but I had to give expression to these feelings of affection and gratitude. I said to them, flushing with exuberance, "I love you. Thank you again." We embraced and our contact ended for that night.

Chapter 10

REBELLION OUTBREAK

It was before daybreak when I began recording everything from the preceding twenty-four hours, almost an hour before the others were up. A little after sunrise Lieutenant Smithson came by and said, "Be ready to load up at 0800 hours, we're headed back to the rear. Pass the word."

"All right!" James sang out. "I do need a shower, some hot grub, and a quart of ice cream." He picked up the radio mic and passed the message on to the squads. We skipped breakfast but heated instant coffee. As we sipped it, Private Mason walked up.

He appeared to be solemn but focused. "Sorry about last night. Thanks for the pills, I got a little rest," he said quietly. "But mostly I laid there and thought about what I could do... if there was anything to make up for shooting her."

He paused a moment and said in complete sincerity, "I've decided to be a Conscientious Objector. That's one thing I can do, never kill anyone else."

We sat there staring up at him in stunned silence. He squatted down, looked me in the eye, and said, "You're a CO. What do I have to do?"

I tried to gather my wits and answer, but then James said, "I'm not sure you can do that after you're already in the war."

Lawrence chimed in, "There is provision for that. I remember reading about it when studying the Selective Service Act."

It struck me that he was making the decision on short notice, and long on emotion, that he hadn't really had time to think it over. "Don't you want to give it some more thought, Ralph? This would be a life-altering move."

He replied immediately and without the least doubt or hesitation, "I don't want to kill anyone else, even if it means I will

68

die or go to prison. Thinking about it more won't change my mind. Just tell me what to do."

I was reluctant to encourage or influence him. But I could see he was honest and not being irrational, "I don't know how it works if someone wants to take CO status after he's been deployed. Lawrence seems to think you can. I had to go before a board of inquiry. They wanted to know if I was against this war or just killing. They asked a lot of questions about my religious beliefs, and whether I would defend my home if it came to that. I remember they asked if I was afraid of combat. There were a lot of questions about moral responsibility and using violence. I had to write an essay for the record."

James said, "We're going back to the rear this morning. Maybe you should make an appointment with the company chaplain."

"Good idea," Lawrence said.

"Have you told anyone else what you want to do?" I asked.

"No," Mason said. "I decided to talk to you first and find out how to apply."

"Maybe you shouldn't tell anyone until you've spoken to the chaplain," I advised.

"All right, I won't. Thanks, Baker. I probably wouldn't have thought of CO, except I knew you're one." He turned and went back to his squad.

"O the hand of fate has started a rebellion in the ranks," Lawrence said with a wry smile. "I'll be a witness at your trial, Private Ernie. I'll testify that you weren't proselytizing or recruiting CO's." James and I chuckled, but I knew the officers would see Ralph's decision as a problem in the ranks.

As we finished coffee, over the radio came the message, "All units, prepare for field evac." We quickly packed our rucks and waited for the bevy of choppers. Soon a roar was heard from the eastern horizon. A smoke grenade was thrown out. It was a relief that we didn't receive incoming fire on the trip back to basecamp.

As soon as we landed, there was a roll call after which we were dismissed for showers and a day without duty. Everyone went to their bunks and stowed their rucks. What a joy it was to clean up after being in the field. I had only been out three days, the others had been in the boonies almost two weeks, soaked in sweat and covered with dirt, smelling like a locker room and wearing stubbly beards.

The rest of the morning I spent on the beach, editing and refining my notes between swims. That afternoon I made a copy and mailed it home, along with a reply to Karen's letter. On the way to the USO for ice cream, Ralph Mason spotted me and ran over. He was with another man from his squad.

"I talked to the chaplain this morning. We prayed about the dead woman, and about being an objector. He wasn't very encouraging, but he said it was my right to apply for CO. He gave me the paperwork. I filled it out and gave it to the company clerk. And I told Sam what I did." Ralph indicated the man at his side.

The man stuck out his hand and said with a friendly smile, "Sammy Smith."

Ralph said, looking me straight in the eyes, "Sam applied too."

"Thanks for leadin' the way," Sammy said. "I always hated killin', but I didn't know about conscious objectin'. The chaplain gave me the papers and Ralph helped me fill 'em out. Back home my daddy taught me it was bad to kill, then the army said we had to. But I don't like it. When I saw them kids yesterday, when we bombed and burned their houses, I knew it weren't right."

Lawrence's words about starting a rebellion in the ranks flashed in my mind. I didn't know whether to congratulate or discourage them. I could foresee a heap of trouble ahead, and that a wave of persecution could be coming for these two—and more for me. One CO in the company might be tolerated, but three? What if there were more? But after a moment's thought I decided then and there, this is a good thing. Not only is killing others the wrong way to settle disagreements, but this war was wrong; we weren't defending our homes and our families from murderous invaders. In fact it seemed that we were the invaders. The generals and the president knew this but there were political and economic forces behind this war, like all wars.

"I can see you two think you're doing the right thing. And you aren't trying to get out of serving. But you know you'll have to go before the officers for a formal hearing on this, don't you?"

"Yeah, the chaplain told me. He said they would ask about faking it. He copied this out of an army book." Ralph said, handing me a piece of paper.

I read it aloud, "For serving personnel of the United States military, conscientious objection applications are subject to an investigative process by a senior officer not in the applicant's chain of command, as well as an interview of the applicant by a military chaplain, as well as a psychiatrist or medical officer."

"Have you told Lieutenant Smithson or Captain Stone?" I asked.

Ralph replied, "No, we haven't seen them. I figured the company clerk would tell the first sergeant, and he would tell the officers."

"Come on, let's have some ice cream," I offered. We headed to the USO and found Lawrence and James already there. We joined them at a table on a shaded deck overlooking the ocean.

James asked Ralph, "Have you seen the chaplain?"

"We did," he answered, indicating Sammy too.

Lawrence perked up, "Both of you are applying for CO status?"

I said, "They are. The chaplain said it was their right. They turned in the paperwork already."

71

Lawrence and James looked at each other, then at us. Lawrence laughed, saying, "Well, this *is* a rebellion. James, what say you? Should we register our displeasure at being forced to carry a weapon?"

James didn't know what to say. Astonishment hung on his face. Ralph and Sammy licked away at their ice cream cones, apparently relieved by the prospect of not having to kill again. I thought about what might be ahead for them. And me. Just then we heard a barrage of out-going artillery followed by jets taking off. This could only mean some troops in the field were engaged in battle; a new round of killing was underway.

"Anybody else want to go for a swim?" Ralph asked.

James said, "Lawrence and I are thinking of going to a movie, 'The Green Beret' is showing at the USO theater. It's a John Wayne flick so it probably won't have any objectors."

That brought a big laugh from Lawrence. He said, "You better join us, Private Baker. It might turn you away from this objector rebellion you've started."

"No thanks," I said. "Think I'd better rest up for the inevitable meeting with our first sergeant." As they went their separate ways, I headed to my bunk for a nap before evening mess. But sleep didn't come. Instead, thoughts about the consequences of Ralph and Sammy's sudden decision to become CO's kept circulating in my head. What would the army do to stop a potential flood of applicants?

Chapter 11

COMMUNION

Just before chowtime, as I lay there wondering what might happen next, the company clerk walked up and said, "Baker, come with me, the first sergeant wants you."

We went into his little office, adjacent to Captain Stone's, and stood at attention. He dismissed the company clerk and said, "At ease, Private Baker. Sit down."

He looked at me for a moment and asked, "Are you aware two men from your platoon requested objector status this morning?"

"Yes, First Sergeant. Mason and Smith."

"Did you have anything to do with their decision?"

"No, First Sergeant. Mason told me this morning, Smith, this afternoon."

"How do you think they arrived at the idea, Private Baker?"

"They both said they don't want to kill any more."

"And you didn't plant the idea in their heads, or in any way encourage them?"

"No, First Sergeant. After they told me they had applied, I said they seemed sincere. But Mason did say that he might not have thought about applying for CO if he hadn't remembered that I was one. He was upset after the death of a woman during yesterday's battle."

"You know, Baker, the army can't fulfill its mission if men won't carry weapons. If I discovered you were counseling men to take objector status I would have to take measures and try to stop it. You understand?"

"Yes, First Sergeant."

73

"Alright Baker, dismissed. Tomorrow Captain Stone and Colonel Simmons may want to see you. Until the company returns to the field, I want you to go back to manning the first-aid tent."

And that's what I did for the next six days. It seemed that the first sergeant believed I purposely influenced Mason and Smith, and maybe others. But, in spite of my concerns, a summons to appear before Stone or Simmons never came. Maybe the first sergeant told them it wouldn't do any good… or that any action by an officer might be seen as suppression.

While I was tending the first-aid tent, my platoon was marched out each morning with metal detectors to clear local roads of landmines. But they had the afternoons off. On the first afternoon, Mason and Smith came by to report that a board of inquiry meeting was set for our last day in the rear.

Ralph said, "We may not have to go out in the field again. It depends on whether we are given CO status. The squad leader told the lieutenant he didn't want men without weapons, that we wouldn't be able to pull night watch, and that he didn't want to be responsible for us."

Then Sammy asked, "What'll that board ask us, Ernie? I'm a little scared to talk to officers. All I know is I don't wanna kill nobody. You think that's enough?"

While I was telling Sammy about my CO hearing, Captain Stone walked by. Evidently, he had overheard some of what was said. His face took on a scowl. We stood at attention and saluted. He returned the salute but continued walking. We realized how this looked. Mason and Smith quickly left in case the captain came back. But he didn't.

That night, as I slept, Joyah and Rayah paid a visit. After enjoying an especially warm and tender embrace, I asked for their insights about Mason and Smith's pending applications for CO. "Do you have any advice about this? You know I didn't actively encourage them. But at the same time, I feel an obligation to at least answer their questions. I'm a little unsure

74

exactly how to handle the situation. I don't really want others to follow them or me. And you know my taking CO status was something personal. I never wanted or planned to become the leader of a rebellion in the ranks. What if others apply, and what if they come to me for advice? Should I not say anything?"

Rayah answered without the least hesitation, "The decisions you now face provide an opening for a lesson on the best way to deal with any confusing or complex situation, one in which the solution is not obvious. We are more Guardians than advisors, but we would have you know there are available to every mortal certain spiritual counselors. These inner influences are actual living spirits who are complements of life as you live it. They are made available by and through the faculty of mind. Ready access to them comes from sincere inner communication and real need."

Joyah continued, saying, "Within you, in your inner life, there exists a divine conspiracy of spiritual influences; they are a gift of Spirit and work as one. They willingly and gladly guide you to the wisdom and truth that are the keys to enriching life and solving difficulties. In fact, they are best known by two words, Wisdom and Truth. They are the source of a supernal understanding that transcends mere human thinking. When you seek within, in sincerity, and in humility, these spiritual influences can offer you the insights needed to resolve any troubling situation."

Rayah added, "Already we spoke to you about the divine entity, the fragment of God, who indwells you. This Indweller helps to spiritualize your thinking. Now we are informing you about the presence of these two additional ministries. The Spirit of Truth and the Spirit of Wisdom work with the indwelling God fragment, always and ever serving in seamless harmony. They are interested in improving your thinking, your wisdom, and your truth-discernment. The quality of your thoughts is what they would improve, along with an expansion of your capacity to love others. Humans can access these Spirits through inner communion. And you should know the only truly effective modes of communion are prayer and worship. Prayer might best be described as conversation with God. Worship should be viewed as intimacy with God."

Joyah went on, "Ernie, for the most part, your spiritual life is undeveloped. You have great compassion for your fellows. And you are doing well in developing your outer life, especially for one so young. But you have not explored the interior regions, your inner life. We would have you develop more trust in the spiritual guidance to which every human has access. Not only will this enrich you, it will provide the wisdom that goes beyond mere opinion, hunches, and guesses. You may have the surety of knowing the right way to do the right thing, once you have full faith and trust in prayer and worship. We admonish you, in your petitions to God, ask for values, not things. Seek for wisdom, courage, patience, and true understanding, not for wish fulfillment. And worship fosters a real relationship with God, which is its own reward."

Rayah asked with great empathy and concern, "Will you consider applying what we have spoken of?"

I was feeling a little sheepish that all this hadn't occurred to me before. Of course, I knew about prayer and worship, but hadn't practiced them much, if at all. Nor had I sought wisdom and truth through them. My religious training had always been more in the background of my interests. I asked, "What are you suggesting I do?"

Joyah replied, "We invite you to commune with us, now." They each offered a hand. I took them.

Rayah began, "Close your eyes and quiet your thoughts." Soon, there was a moment without thinking, then a feeling of *light*—that's the only way to describe it—came to me. I also felt an intimate connection with these two angels. It was extremely beautiful, like a feeling but more. Nothing needed to be said. At that moment, it seemed as though all my questions would find answers, and that everything was in harmony. The experience was *very* peaceful and I'm not sure how long it lasted.

And then Joyah spoke ever so softly, "Father, it is with great joy that we come to you with the one we are guarding, in worship and praise of you. Your bounty is limitless and your love is fathomless. For these gifts, we thank you. Receive us Father, in your embrace." Then—I will never forget—time and space seemed to vanish, and all of everything came to rest. A harmony of connectedness, a wave of belonging to the entire universe settled around us. Somehow, I could sense an immense love, without and within. Finally, I grasped the meaning of, "That peace which passes all understanding" and hoped never to forget or neglect this knowing, this connection with Spirit. The experience was pivotal. Never after that did I doubt the existence of God, or the love of God.

Then Rayah and Joyah returned me to sleep. I dreamed of visiting the Paradise they had spoken of, that I met God and received a divine embrace. I heard the words, "This is my child, in whom I am well pleased." Nothing ever sounded so good.

I was jarred from sleep by the sound of sirens and yells of "Incoming!" A few seconds later there were loud explosions nearby. Everyone was scrambling to the nearest bunker in underwear, helmets, and unlaced boots–my comrades with their weapons and me with a med-pouch. We watched as several parachute flares were sent up, and saw helicopters lift off and move out of the area. The attack stopped after about five minutes.

There were about fifteen of us in the bunker, including Lawrence and James. Lawrence said with his usual detachment, "That's just Charlie giving us a wake-up call." It was nearing sun-up. After a short while the sirens stopped, and we went back to our bunks and finished dressing.

James went out to survey the damage. He came back and said, "Looks like they were aiming for the ammo dump. Thank God they missed."

Before breakfast I wrote everything in the journal I could remember since the last entry.

Chapter 12

WARNING

For the remainder of the week in the rear, the angels didn't visit. I stayed busy from after breakfast until sundown, treating the company's many little ailments. On the next to the last day, another letter from Karen arrived. Her gallery presentation netted excellent reviews and three works were sold at an impressive price. Best of all, another show was scheduled. I sorely wished to be there. I missed her, and being at school.

The last day before the company was scheduled to return to the field, Mason and Smith had their hearing. Afterward they came by the first-aid tent.

Ralph said, "Good news! We were both granted CO status. The officers in charge didn't even give us a hard time. They looked at our applications and asked a bunch of questions. Then they made us leave. After fifteen minutes, the company clerk told us they voted OK."

Sammy was gleeful. He offered thanks, shaking my hand, smiling, and saying, "We got hospital duty, Ernie! We don't hafta carry a gun no more."

Ralph added, "For the rest of our tour we're assigned to the base clinic. We'll carry stretchers, get supplies, and whatever else they need."

"Have you told the lieutenant yet?" I asked.

"We did... and he wasn't very happy," Ralph answered. "All he said was that he's ordering up two more to replace us."

"When do you go to work?"

Sammy said, "Tomorrah. I ain't never worked in a hospital. But it's gotta be better'n humpin' a ruck all day. It's all 'cause of you, Ernie."

I congratulated them. They headed to the USO for ice cream. As they walked away I stood there marveling at the interesting turn of events. It was good Ralph and Sam wouldn't have to do any more killing; they might have less post-war trauma. And their chances of surviving would be much better working at the base hospital. But this meant their replacements would have to do the job from which they were excused. The war would go on, with little notice—unless there were more applications for CO status. No sooner had I thought that than several others from my platoon showed up. Obviously, the news about Ralph and Sammy had gotten around.

Looking at their faces, something told me a dam had burst. "We heard you helped Mason and Smith get CO," one of them said. "Can you help us?"

Apparently, because of Ralph and Sammy, I was now saddled with the role of CO counselor, and there was no use trying to convince anyone otherwise. I said, "Look guys, helping men get CO status is not a job I asked for. All I can tell you is that if you apply for CO, you'll have to go before a board of officers and convince them you're being truthful, and not just trying to get out of field duty. Mason and Smith went through the process this morning. Talk to them, they're at the USO."

Hearing that, they left. Evidently, Lawrence's prediction was coming true. I wondered where it might stop. What if the whole platoon applied for CO? What if this spread to other platoons, even the whole company and beyond?

After finishing up the day at the aid tent, I went to the mess hall for a meal, then to my bunk. Most of the platoon was there, having a lively discussion about Ralph and Sammy's change of status. It was immediately obvious the majority favored it.

When Lawrence saw me, he said, "All hail! A saint is in our presence." A cheer went up. I felt my face flush, and a bit of uncertainty mixed with resentment. I really didn't want this role as CO rebellion leader, but it seemed inevitable and unavoidable.

I looked around and asked, "Who all is going to apply for CO?"

A loud voice from the back of the tent rang out, "I'm not!" Two others said, "Me neither."

Another man stood and said, "You guys joined up. We were drafted! I never asked to kill women and kids, and burn down villages. It's not right. And everybody knows we're not winning the war. I don't see any reason not to go for CO status." The enlisted men frowned but didn't say anything. And then we noticed the lieutenant standing at the tent's entrance. Evidently, he'd been listening. We snapped to attention.

He walked down the center aisle looking us over, and then yelled angrily, "Get some shut-eye, first platoon. We move out at 0630 tomorrow. Baker, come with me."

He led the way out to a bench facing the ocean and ordered me to "Have a seat." After a minute he said, "Private, when you arrived I told you to keep your nose clean. Now you seem to be leading a CO uprising in my platoon. I am not happy about it and the army is not happy about it. I want to know what you're going to do to change that."

"Sir, I haven't encouraged anyone to apply for CO. But I can sense their sincerity in not wanting to kill anymore. The ones who asked me just wanted to know what questions an inquiry board would ask. I tried *not* to encourage them."

"I find that hard to believe, Private. Why are they cheering and calling you a saint?"

"The platoon knew I was a CO when I got here. After Mason and Smith were given CO status, that was enough to land me in that role, one I never asked for."

He was quiet and thoughtful for a minute. Then he said, "I'm ordering you not to say any more about your status, or to give out *any* information on how to apply for CO. Is that understood?"

"Yes, sir."

"If I hear that you've disobeyed, there will be consequences. Dismissed."

He remained on the bench. I went back to my bunk. Even in the dark I could tell everyone was looking at me. They knew the lieutenant had probably dressed me down about the CO business and told me to shut up. Nothing was said, but the tension between the draftees and the joiners filled the air. It took a while to get to sleep. Just before daybreak I had a long, involved dream about being court-martialed for treason.

That morning we went to the mess hall for breakfast and then collected rations to make ready to leave. This time the company marched to the field rather than airlifting out. After more than ten klicks we stopped for a noontime meal under the shade of a clump of trees by a dry creek bed. James, Lawrence, and I sat together. The lieutenant went to lunch with Captain Stone.

As we ate, about a dozen men from the fourth platoon came up. One of them said to me, "We heard two guys in first platoon got CO status yesterday, and that you came to Nam as a CO."

Before I could answer, James said, "Yep, Mason and Smith are back in the rear, working hospital duty. You thinking of applying?"

The man replied, "We're wondering if anyone can be a CO, and what we have to do."

James replied, "Mason and Smith made an appointment with the chaplain. Five days later they were CO's. They had to fill out forms and answer some questions from officers about their beliefs."

Another of the group asked, "You mean religious beliefs?"

Lawrence chimed in, "Gentlemen, the army wants to know whether CO applicants are honest in their request, religious or not. They would like to know if you are, God forbid, merely trying to get out of field duty. You draftees wouldn't want to acquire CO status simply to avoid combat, would you? Who doesn't love carrying ninety pounds on your back day-in and day-out in the tropical heat for a year, all the while eating canned food left over from the last war, being shot at, and dancing around booby traps?" That brought a chuckle of agreement from the group.

Whether or not to heed the lieutenant's warning was going through my mind. All I could think to say was, "I've been ordered not to talk about CO status."

James said somewhat indignantly, "I wasn't ordered. Ernie applied for it before he came to Nam. It's a soldier's right, even after they are in a war zone."

They thanked us and went back to their platoon. A few minutes later the lieutenant returned and said the company would be going to a little village two kilometers away, on a search-and-destroy mission. There were intelligence reports it was a VC stronghold.

We loaded up and marched out with the apprehension of combat. The midday equatorial sun was blazing, with little breeze to evaporate the profuse sweat. After about an hour we arrived at the village and surrounded it. Each man dug a foxhole in the dry rice paddies, behind a dike. While we were digging in, several groups of villagers carrying belongings tried to leave. They were searched and turned back. No one was permitted to exit.

Chapter 13

SEARCH AND DESTROY

That afternoon half of each platoon was ordered into the village. The other half remained to hold the perimeter. Lawrence, James, and I followed the lieutenant in. No resistance was encountered. The villagers were gathered at its center. There were several elderly women, two old men, and a dozen or so pre-teen children. Some protested, one very old woman complained vigorously, shouting at us as she cried. Most simply wept in fear and cringed with apprehension. After the villagers—about twenty in all—were assembled and put under guard, a hut-to-hut search began.

We three stayed with the lieutenant as the squads spread out and began the search. Very soon we heard over the radio, "Third squad reporting, we have a tunnel." Lieutenant Smithson took the mic from James and ordered, "Hold your position. Don't go in, there could be traps." Then to us, he said, "Let's have a look."

We walked about a hundred yards to the hut where third squad was searching. In one corner, there was a hole that had been covered by a bed on a bamboo frame. The lieutenant shined a flashlight looking for tripwires and hidden punji pits. He called the squad leader and ordered him to send one of his men into the tunnel. The leader chose one of the three who had volunteered to join the army, and who had declared their opposition to applying for CO status the previous night.

"Watch out for wires and pits, corporal, and not just at the entrance," The lieutenant told him.

"Yes, sir. I will," he said with willingness and confidence.

Lawrence and James helped lower him in. The hole was about six feet deep. It opened into a larger horizontal tunnel at the bottom. He moved slowly and cautiously, shining his light in

83

all directions before each step. The lieutenant asked, "What do you see, Corporal?"

"Nothing yet, sir." A moment later, he yelled, "tripwire!"

"Come out of there, Corporal!" Smithson ordered. When the man returned to the tunnel's entrance, Lawrence and James lifted him out. "What did you find?"

"Sir, there's a wire and a punji pit about ten feet in."

"Get Stone." James changed the radio channel to the company frequency and handed the mic to the lieutenant. He said, "We have a tunnel with a pit. There may be mines too."

The reply came back, "Hold your position, first platoon. Fourth and second platoons also have tunnels."

Then we heard an explosion. A strong poof of wind blew out of the tunnel entrance our platoon was searching. A dust and smoke cloud went up where the second platoon was searching. There was yelling. I could hear, "Medic!"

Over the radio, we heard Captain Stone say, "Hold your positions. Don't search the tunnels." Then we heard Stone's radioman call for a medivac chopper.

"Stay here," the lieutenant told us. He ran toward the dust cloud.

"They must be connected," James said. "We're lucky that blast didn't set off a mine in our tunnel." We three moved out of the hut along with the man who had gone down our tunnel entrance. He was shaking and sweating profusely. I offered him water. He took a long drink.

The explosion had caused a stir in the group of villagers; some were wailing and shouting. They knew this would cast suspicion and blame on them. Just then another, and very loud, explosion came from the opposite side of the village. More yelling could be heard from both soldiers and villagers. Again, we heard a cry of, "Medic!"

The lieutenant returned, and we heard Captain Stone over the radio, "All platoons, return to your positions on the perimeter!"

"You heard him," Lieutenant Smithson said to us, then shouted, "Back to the perimeter, first platoon—now!" James repeated the order over the radio.

As we moved out, yellow smoke went up where the first explosion occurred. We could see a medivac about to land amid the huts. It stayed on the ground several minutes.

When we were back on the perimeter, James asked the lieutenant, "How many were hurt, sir?"

"In second platoon one was injured, one was buried. They were trying to dig him out when the other mine went off."

James said, "The second one probably hit more men. It didn't sound like it was underground. That medivac must be waiting for the injured." As he said that the chopper lifted off. We could see it had several wounded, maybe dead, on board.

"Tell the platoon to stay here," Smithson said to James, then he ran toward the captain's position. James relayed the order over the radio.

"What now?" I asked.

Lawrence answered, "The mission is search and destroy. We searched." It took a second to realize what he was saying.

James pointed to the east and said, "Here they come." Jets could be heard approaching. He picked up the radio mic and yelled, "Take cover!"

As bombs began to fall, screams came out of the village. One jet after another dropped two-ton bombs intended to collapse tunnels. They were followed by napalm. After twenty or more had fallen, the outcries stopped. Another twenty were dropped which completely obliterated the village. No hut was left standing. Black smoke rose from several places inside.

When the sorties ceased, we remained in place, observing. Two more explosions were heard during the next half hour.

Lawrence said, "Those are probably mines cooking off." We stayed in place for another hour, until no more explosions were heard. The order came to go back in and search the village, or what was left of it. Again, half the men remained on the perimeter.

The smell of recently detonated explosives was overwhelming. The sight of bodies, young and old, dead and torn, was beyond sickening. Between bomb craters we could see collapsed tunnels. They were everywhere in the village. The body of the soldier who was buried was found. A chopper came to take it to the rear.

An order from Stone came over the radio, "Let's get a body count, platoon leaders. Each one search a quarter of the village."

I felt a terrible frustration with war. One body, ours, got special treatment. The other bodies were ignored, except to be reported as enemy dead. In truth, they were the children and old folks. No NVA or VC, and no weapons were found.

On the way back, I asked the lieutenant, "Are those bodies going to be left out, sir?"

He looked at me with a mix of contempt and anger. "Those are VC conspirators, private. You saw the village was riddled with tunnels. And we lost at least one man. What do you want the army to do?"

"Are you saying those villagers will be reported as enemies?" I asked.

"Yes, Baker. Those tunnels didn't dig themselves."

"But, sir, we don't know for a fact that those kids and old people were VC. And they couldn't have been NVA."

"At ease, Private Baker! We do know..." But then a call

86

came over the radio to meet with the captain. As he left, he ordered James, "Have the men chow down and set up watch."

After he was out of earshot, James said, "That's the kind of day that leaves me without much appetite." We blew up our air mattresses as the sun set. The sky was a stunning mix of red, orange, and purple, now admixed with black smoke still rising from the smoldering village.

"Do you think those villagers were VC," I asked James and Lawrence. "Shouldn't we have removed the civilians before we bombed the village? How can they be counted as enemy kills? Some of them weren't more than six years old."

"Such is war," Lawrence declared with a definite but detached sadness.

James said, "I agree with you, Ernie. We should have let them out before the bombing. We're only making more enemies when we massacre whole villages."

As we sat there watching the beautiful sunset, one of the men who had been ordered to search the villagers' bodies walked up. He was from our platoon. He looked pale and distraught.

"You OK?" I asked.

"No. I can't do this anymore," he replied. "Those kids..." He tried to hold it back, but he broke down and sobbed, unable to complete the sentence. When he regained some composure, he said haltingly, "I was thinking all day about applying for CO... Then this happened... I can't be a part of it anymore. Those little kids didn't deserve to be killed. Tell me what I have to do to get CO."

James said, "I'll tell the lieutenant. Ernie, give him a couple of those pills. Try to get some rest, Private. I'll ask your squad leader to relieve you from night guard."

I handed him two sedatives and tried to comfort him. "Do like James says, try to get some shut-eye. I'll talk to the lieutenant about getting you back to the rear." He sniffed, and with shaky hands took the pills, then headed toward his squad's position.

"That's one more for your CO rebellion, Private Ernie," Lawrence said.

"It's not mine," I shot back.

It was cooling down a bit. We made hot chocolate while twilight turned to night. As we took the first sips, the lieutenant came by.

He said to James, "Inform the squad leaders we're going back to the rear in the morning." We all three looked at him with the obvious question.

James asked it, "Why? We've only been out one day."

"I know that, Corporal. Captain Stone is putting the company on stand-down. Twenty-five men have said they want to apply for CO status. We can't stay in the field when one quarter of the company isn't willing to carry a weapon. It appears you've disobeyed my orders, Baker."

James spoke up, "Sir, Ernie didn't say anything, I did. Some men came to us during lunch break today and asked about CO status. I told them to see a chaplain. And one more from our platoon just told us he wants to apply."

Smithson looked at James and me as if we were conspirators. He said, "Evidently the word has spread, Corporal. Thanks to you two we are now a non-functioning unit. You can expect to face an inquiry when we get back to the rear." He turned and headed toward Stone's position.

Lawrence said with a bit of smile, "Well! Seems we have a situation here. What do you think, James, shall we join the rebellion?"

"I think we better, now that you mention it," James replied. "My dad is *not* going to like it, but what we're doing here isn't right. The more we kill the more we will have to kill. Massacring old folks and little kids is not going to win the war."

88

Lawrence said, "Why not take CO status? I must confess I'm not that fond of the killing. Indeed, it goes against my philosophy, which does allow defense of home and family. But that doesn't seem to be the case here. In fact, we're destroying someone else's home and family, someone who poses no threat to me and mine."

I was speechless. I wasn't sure what to think or do. Had I really fomented a rebellion? It wasn't my intention. But I certainly understood how these men felt.

The next morning, after breakfast, we were airlifted out then sent to our quarters to wait for orders.

Chapter 14

REBELLION AND REVELATION

While we waited, an angry debate broke out between the draftees and the three volunteers. There was plenty of arguing about whether the war was being won or lost. At one point two men had to be restrained. Squad leaders stepped in to calm the tempers.

When it was all over the draftees who hadn't already declared they wanted to apply for CO status did so. That meant the entire platoon, with the exception of the three army recruits, wanted to opt out of carrying weapons.

We broke up into small groups after the intense debate. Among the draftees who wanted to apply for CO, there were discussions about what might happen next. It wasn't long until Lieutenant Smithson and a chaplain entered the tent. Everyone came to attention. The lieutenant said, "At ease, first platoon. This is Captain Thurbon, headquarters' chaplain. He wants to see everyone who is applying for CO. The rest of you are dismissed." There was a moment of hesitation and then the three recruits walked out. The shock on the lieutenant's face was unmistakable. No doubt he wondered what had happened to turn the rest of the platoon to applying. The chaplain looked a bit shocked as well. Smithson cast a disapproving scowl my way.

Captain Thurbon seized the moment and said in clear voice, "Men, what you're contemplating has serious consequences. If you believe that applying for CO will get you out of duty in the field, you may be disappointed. If you think this will get you sent back stateside, you might want to think again. Let's look at some of the consequences of being a CO, like how you will be seen by the army, and by your families. It will likely disrupt relationships with members of your church. If you apply, even if it's not granted, it will go on your permanent record, it will follow you long after your hitch in the army is over. If you are granted CO status your family could be adversely affected. They could be isolated or even persecuted. You may very well be labeled a coward by neighbors. And there is a good chance you will lose some friends. I would advise you to reconsider before applying. Such a move on your part might seem like a good idea in the heat of battle, but in the long term, you could very much regret it." He hesitated a moment to let his warnings sink in. He looked around. No one recanted. Finally he asked, "Are there questions?"

"What do we have to do to apply, and what will happen?" James asked. Thurbon looked at him as if to say, "Haven't you heard anything I just said?"

After a long look at the faces around him, the chaplain answered, "Privates Mason and Smith came before me and the board of inquiry two days ago and were granted CO status. They were required to convince the board of their sincerity, and their willingness to accept the consequences, and to put their reasons for objecting into writing. Everyone who still wants to apply, add your name to this list." He handed a clipboard to the man standing closest. No minds had changed; every man present signed the list. At that point Lieutenant Smithson left without saying a word, but his disgust and disappointment were obvious.

When the list was complete Thurbon said, "I will arrange a board of inquiry and inform Captain Stone. He will let you know when and where. And I should add that if you change your mind, and want your name removed from this list, you may at any time." He turned to walk out. James called us to attention.

When he was gone one man said emphatically, "I'm not changing my mind." That brought a chorus of agreement.

Just then the company clerk appeared at the tent's doorway saying, "Orders from Captain Stone... You're confined here until 1200 hours. You may go to the mess hall, and only the mess hall. You will have one hour to eat. Report back here by 1300 hours and remain until evening chow. You will have one hour for chow, from 1800 until 1900 hours. After chow confine yourselves here until tomorrow. After breakfast, you will be assigned to camp garbage detail." He turned and left.

A collective moan arose. Lawrence was the first to speak, "Looks like consequences are upon us gentlemen. Woe be to them who lay down their arms in the midst of war."

"That may not be the only consequence," James added. But we weren't deprived of mail. The company clerk came back during the afternoon with letters and packages.

I spent the rest of the day updating and editing the journal. The others wrote letters, read books, played cards, or tried to sleep. Mason and Smith were asked many questions about going before the board of inquiry. The general feeling was upbeat, but there was a lot of talk about how stupid and tragic the war was, and how the truth was being suppressed or distorted. That evening, a man from another platoon was persuaded to bring us four gallons of ice cream from the USO. It was spooned into canteen cups and consumed along with cookies and other goodies several men had received from home.

That night there was another visit with the angels. It felt very good to be in their presence again. The contrast between the waking hours and the nocturnal visits with my Guardians could hardly have been more stark. This visit, like the others, began with a hug, during which I felt what could only be called radiant love. And their embrace seemed to set the stage for what followed. After being in their arms I felt completely open, receptive, and attentive. This, I believe, helped me recall what they said, word for word.

Rayah began, saying, "Ernie, we watch the unfolding of your life experience with fascination. We know you face challenging circumstances and complex decisions. And we would encourage you to remember what we spoke of regarding the use of prayer and worship. Prayer provides a venue for asking questions. Worship yields creative solutions. If you will utilize this potent combination of prayer and worship in daily life, you will find there is less uncertainty and more satisfaction. Make time each day for this. Make it a habit to go within. You will discover that the more often you do so, the easier access becomes. These inner resources, available to all humanity, are too little known and vastly under-used. The insights you gain can be of tremendous worth and inestimable value. And each episode of inner communion strengthens your connection to wisdom, to truth, and to God."

I decided right then, to heed their advice and take time out every day, to connect with those "inner resources." I felt a little ashamed for having ignored their previous advice about prayer and worship. "I will," I said. "The way things are going, some clarity and certainty will go a long way. I keep wondering what my role should be in this objector rebellion…"

Joyah replied, "That, Ernie, would be an excellent opening question for prayer."

"Yeah, I guess it would. I promise to give it a try."

"Excellent!" Rayah exclaimed. "Tonight, we want to offer more revelations which, we hope, you will someday share. Already have we given you a preview of Mansion One. Now we would reveal more about the career of ascending souls. You will recall there are seven mansion worlds that comprise the first heaven; they are but the first stations on the long journey to the Paradise abode of the Universal Father. And even when you reach the Father of All, eternity lies beyond. Gradually, very gradually, you will be made aware that the Universe of Universes is virtually without limits."

Joyah added, "And although astronomy and science have not yet recognized it, the universe has a center. This is the dwelling place of the Deity that humanity refers to as God, the one we refer to as the Universal Father. God is the First Source and Center of all things and beings. All ascending beings are taught that Paradise is where the Father is personally present, notwithstanding that he indwells you this very minute. It is God's prerogative to be in more than one place at the same time, in fact numberless places. This fact may be difficult for mortals to fathom, but it remains forever true. Because of this ability to be everywhere at once, it is also true that nothing escapes the notice of the creator of the universe. Nothing. Never forget, God is perfectly omniscient."

Rayah went on, "All ascenders will sometime learn that God the Father constantly pours forth spirit and energy. Spirit and energy are what personalize and propel the vast cosmos of inhabited galaxies, nebulas, and worlds. Earth is but one of countless worlds on which life has been planted. And only the Universal Father knows how many worlds there are. We also want to assure you that the cosmos is well organized. The Father of Persons and the creator of the universes could supervise all of everything, but that is not the way things are. God is the great delegator. Everything that can be delegated is. Knowing something of the structure and hierarchy of the army, it should not be difficult for you to see that the head of the army does not do everything. He delegates both duty and authority. He may be aware of what is transpiring at every level, but he does not personally do everything that is done."

"Are you saying the universe has Generals, Colonels, Majors, Captains, Lieutenants, and Sergeants that have duties and responsibilities in running things?"

Joyah answered, "We are saying the universe is vast and far more complex than any human has imagined. The armies of heaven are designed for the progressive attainment of the creatures who inhabit it. Set in your mind now that the universes are not static; that all inhabited worlds progress by gradual evolution—physical, social, and spiritual evolution. The Heavenly Father has both a purpose and a goal. And the armies of administrators and angels who are assigned on spiritual missions do not fight one another... they teach, supervise, and coordinate in sublime harmony, always and ever integrated in one diverse but unified ministry. The universe is truly one great school. And while human ignorance and acrimony prevails here, divine truth, beauty, and goodness is the way of heaven. One day, Earth will attain that high harmony.

"The teaching method of the heavenly spheres is that those ahead instruct those just behind. You are not considered to be in possession of knowledge until you have demonstrated a willingness and an ability to pass that knowledge on. This heavenly plan of ceaseless progress must be administered. The Universal Father could perform all administrative duties, enact and prosecute all orders, but that would deprive vast hosts of beings both purpose and experience. As you ascend, more responsibilities will be assigned to you, along with greater freedoms. But never will such tasks be beyond your level of knowledge and ability. Therefore, we encourage you to begin now... to take the reins of responsibility, to seize the opportunity to serve in ever higher offices, and thereby earn more and more freedom to expand your spirit and explore the universe."

There was so much to absorb but I had to ask, "Are you saying I should step out in front and lead the objectors?"

Rayah replied earnestly, "That is for you to decide but there is no better teacher than raw, living experience. And we have already urged you to seek advice and counsel in prayer, to seek creative solutions in worship."

"I see... I'd better take some time to think about what to do. In fact, I'll try what you suggest, with prayer."

"Good!" they said in perfect unison, then reached out to hug me. My next memory was waking up to reveille blasting over the camp speakers.

Chapter 15

BAKER'S BRIGADE

Right after reveille, Lieutenant Smithson appeared at the tent's entrance saying in a booming voice, "First platoon! After mess, report back here at 0730 hours for trash detail. You're still confined to this tent except for showers and chow." He turned and marched off. Much grumbling followed, after which we put on fatigues, laced our boots and headed for the mess hall. James, Lawrence, me, and several others from first platoon were eating and having coffee when five men from another company came and sat at our table.

One of them said, "We heard your platoon had CO's. We were up late talking about the war, and whether or not to try for CO status. We want to apply. What do we have to do?"

Lawrence chuckled and said, "More volunteers for your objector's brigade, Private Baker."

"What brigade?" the man asked.

James answered, "The way it's going, there may be a brigade of CO's. Day before yesterday about a dozen men from fourth platoon said they wanted to apply for CO. All but three men in our platoon are applying, including me. Now you guys. Hey, maybe we should call it Baker's Brigade."

Lawrence joked, "Yeah, our mission can be to search and destroy garbage."

"Garbage...?" one of them asked.

James replied, "All the CO applicants drew garbage detail this morning. In fact, we'd better get back and start hauling."

As we left, I said to the five, "If you want to apply for CO, put in a request to see the company chaplain."

James added with a laugh, "We can use the help taking out the trash."

96

At 0730 all the objector applicants were told to leave their weapons on their bunks and load up on the waiting trucks. We were driven a couple of kilometers to the other end of the basecamp. A staff sergeant there ordered us to fall in. As we stood at attention the smell of burning garbage filled our nostrils. Not far away a backhoe was digging a hole to bury the ashes.

The sergeant said, "At ease. Welcome slackers. The army, in its infinite wisdom, has decided that them who won't carry a weapon can carry the garbage. I take it ya'll are draftees? Any of you volunteers? No one? My, oh my, what is this man's army coming to? All right, let's get down and dirty. Who here is qualified to drive a deuce-and-a-half? I need six drivers. This detail has two lovely positions, drivers and swampers. Drivers drive and swampers load. If you can drive, raise your hand and keep it up." He picked six out and had them move away from the others. We others were divided into six groups and each group was assigned a driver. Each driver was given a map of the basecamp with his territory outlined in red.

"All right, men. Load up and head to your assigned area, go by every tent, shack, and hut. Put every barrel you find on the truck. When you have a full load, bring 'em here and dump 'em. Take the empty barrels back to their point of origin and get another load. Repeat until every bit of trash has been rescued and deposited on the burn pit. Any questions?"

Lawrence asked, "Will we receive the Meritorious Garbage Cross for our service?"

Everyone laughed.

"Yes, Corporal," the sergeant shot back, "With a double maggot cluster. Now move out! And take a lunch break at 1200 hours... if you still have an appetite."

It was an appetite-killing assignment. Tropical heat makes quick work of fermenting garbage. It took most of the day to gather and dump all the barrels in our territory, after which a shower and a change of clothes eliminated most, but not all the stench.

97

That evening Smithson came to the tent with new orders. We snapped to attention as he entered. He looked around and said, "At ease. All CO applicants will report to company HQ at 0800 hours day after tomorrow. You will each go before a panel of officers to determine whether your application will be accepted or rejected. Anyone who has changed his mind, step forward now." No one moved. The lieutenant gave it a minute, searching the group for any who might be wavering. Still no one moved.

"Baker, Mason, Smith, you already have CO status. Follow me." After we were outside he said, "So far, forty-four applications for CO have been submitted. Mason and Smith, you have your assignment as hospital flunkies. Report for duty. Dismissed." They departed. "Baker, the captain has issued orders that you will have three areas of responsibility: garbage detail, mess hall helpers, and latrine maintenance. You will take charge of all CO applicants and assign them to an area upon request of the officers in charge. But you're still under my command. If there's any trouble, you will have me to deal with. Understood?"

"Yes, sir."

"For the time being you and your men are confined to the tent, except when on duty, at chow, or showering. Any questions?"

I said, "Sir, some of the men who are applying for CO out-rank me."

"That's been taken care of. Private Baker, from now on, you're a buck sergeant. Dismissed."

I went back in the tent feeling somewhat shocked at being promoted over others, some who had been in-country much longer. At the same time, I felt dread at having to be the camp's delegator of dirty duties, manned by a growing group of objectors.

James asked, "What did he say?"

98

"I'm a sergeant now, in charge of camp garbage, mess hall mops, and toilets."

Lawrence patted me on the back saying, "Congrats, Sergeant Baker! You are moving up in this man's army, even though you didn't get laundry detail." I smiled at him weakly.

James said with noticeable sadness, "Now we know the consequences of refusing to carry a weapon. Oh well, just nine months to go. Can't wait 'til my dad hears about this assignment... If it's all the same to you, Ernie, I volunteer for mess hall duty."

All the implications began to dawn on me. I was going to have to assign and corral forty-four men, maybe more, for unpleasant work, probably for the rest of my tour. And I wouldn't be a medic anymore.

Before lights-out everyone in the tent had heard about "the consequences." But no one changed their mind. I lay in my bunk wishing to be back home, going to classes every day, and spending carefree weekends with Karen. Never could I have foreseen where this CO thing would lead. And I wondered how it might play out.

Sometime during the night Joyah and Rayah appeared. They were well aware of my slumping attitude over being promoted to sergeant of the flies. After a hug from them, Joyah said in a soft and consoling voice, "Don't let your countenance fall over such trivialities, Ernie. Look on this as an opportunity. See it as a challenge. One of the greatest lessons, in this life, and the next, is teamwork. You have been given a team—so learn how to manage it. The nature of the work is of little importance, the lessons to be had are of great importance."

I realized she was right, and that I was thinking only of myself. "Will there be garbage duty on the mansion worlds?" They laughed. That laugh was enough to lift my spirits.

"On the mansions, no duty is looked down upon. All work has dignity and value. Every service is a necessary part of the functioning of the whole," Rayah assured me. "And teamwork has its rewards. You will find nothing quite so satisfying as harmonious cooperation with your fellows in achieving some worthy goal. Those tasks to which you and your fellows have been assigned may be seen as having little or no value, but without such unpleasant chores, like garbage removal, all organizations would quickly break down. It does not take a far-seeing mind to realize that disease and disorder would threaten the very progress of civilization were it not for garbage collection. The world may look down on such work, but the heavens do not."

Joyah added, "No team can function smoothly, or produce good results, without intelligent leadership. After you reach the mansion worlds, you will discover that very few enterprises are accomplished by one individual. And the higher you ascend the more you will appreciate and value those with whom you work. All progressing mortals will learn to be both leader and follower... and that a good leader is also a good follower."

Chapter 16

INCURSION

I was jarred out of the meeting with Rayah and Joyah by rifle fire, coming from the east. Then a big, BOOOOM! The shock wave from the explosion nearly shook us out of our bunks. We heard someone yell, "Satchel charge!" Friendly and enemy fire was being exchanged. Evidently the camp perimeter had been breached on the ocean side. More yelling and weapon fire was heard. The camp siren went silent, as did the generator. All was dark except for faint moonlight. Everyone grabbed his flashlight and scrambled to the nearest bunker.

As we were running, there was a call for a medic in the direction of the firefight. I went back to my bunk for the med-pouch. "Medic!" came another call. Bullets were flying. Frantic yelling cut the air. I was scared to the bone as I ran toward the call for help. There was just enough moonlight to see so I turned off my flashlight in order not be a target. But I tripped over a rock, fell, and got a face-full of sand.

"Medic!" came a louder, even more desperate call. Just as I stood up a ricocheting bullet grazed the outside of my left forearm. I panicked for a second, but then realized it wasn't a deep wound. Once again, "Medic!" I resumed running, crouching as much as possible.

I approached the back of a bunker where I thought the call for help originated. Fire from rifles and a machine gun was going out toward the invaders. The sound was deafening. I stayed low and called as loud as I could, "I'm a medic."

"In here!" someone yelled. I quickly crawled to the bunker's back entrance and went in. There was a man with blood gushing from his right hand and right leg.

I took out a long piece of thin rubber tubing, quickly cut it in half and handed one to the man next to me. "Do what I do," I ordered.

101

While I applied the tourniquet to the leg, he did so with the hand. I looked around and noticed another man down. I shined a light in his face. He was gone, shot in the neck.

Three men ran out of the bunker. Those remaining kept firing. After a minute, we heard several grenades explode. The enemy fire stopped and someone yelled, "Cease fire!" After a minute with no more firing or explosions we heard the order, "Hold your positions." Then, "We got 'em."

After another minute or two of relative quiet the injured man groaned, "My leg." I administered a shot of morphine, then wrote an 'M' on his forehead.

"We have to get this man to the hospital," I said.

One of the men peering out the front of the bunker yelled, "We have wounded, Sergeant. All clear?"

"Move 'em out," came the reply. One of the men in the bunker made a radio call for an ambulance. Two others helped me carry the wounded man out to the roadway, fifty yards behind the bunker. He was still hurting but not complaining. As we waited I spoke words of assurance that he would be all right, and probably be sent home as a result of his wounds. He replied in agonized jest, "Will I get one Purple Heart or two?" His leg and hand weren't bleeding much but they were turning blue below the tourniquets. Just then the ambulance approached. It had two other wounded men on board. Aides jumped out, loaded our man on board, and took off.

We three went back to the bunker to retrieve the body of the dead man. It was loaded onto a jeep and they took it to the camp morgue. I trudged back to my bunk and looked at my wound. The sleeve was blood-soaked. My arm had a long deep slice that needed stitching. The sun was rising and my tent mates were returning. Lawrence offered to drive me to the hospital.

As I waited outside, several officers could be heard discussing the incursion. One said, "There were six of them. They snuck onto the beach in a sampan. We found it near where they were killed. My sergeant said it was an alert bunker guard who spotted them and started firing. One of them had a satchel charge. He ran toward the bunker to blow it up, but was shot down before he could get there. The satchel went off. The other five were pinned down by fire from the two closest bunkers. A guard in one of the bunkers finished them off with grenades. We lost one man, three more were injured. The three will make it."

"Ernie!" I looked around to see who called my name. It was Ralph; he saw the blood and bandage. "What happened?" he asked. "You injured again?" I showed him the wound. He led me into a partitioned area where small wounds were treated.

A nurse walked in and smiled, saying, "What have we here, Ralph? Get a suture kit, will ya?" She looked at my nametag. "You get caught in that skirmish on the beach, Baker?" Ralph returned and handed her the kit.

"I did." She injected my arm with painkiller and then excused herself while the medicine took effect.

Ralph sat down and said, "You got off easy. They're prepping the three who were wounded for surgery. We heard one didn't make it. At least those commandos didn't get to the ammo dump."

"How's Sammy doing?" I asked.

"He likes this duty. We don't have it bad. We work all night and have all day to ourselves. Twelve on, twelve off. How's things with first platoon? We heard a bunch more applied for CO." I updated him about what all had happened; that the growing group of CO's were now garbage men, kitchen police, and toilet tenders. And that I was the assigned leader of "Baker's Brigade." He laughed. I was happy to see that he seemed to have made peace with the killing of the village woman. He said with deep sincerity, "I'm glad to be here at the hospital, helping hurt people."

The nurse came back and sewed up my arm. She sent Ralph to set up the next patient. As he left he said with a gentle smile, "Looks like you'll be getting another Purple Heart. Come by and see me and Sammy sometime when you aren't wounded. Ice cream's on me."

The nurse bandaged my arm and said to return to duty. I hitched a ride back to the tent. Lieutenant Smithson was there. He looked at the bandage and asked, "You fit for duty?"

"Yes, sir."

"I heard about last night, Sergeant Baker. I'll put you in for Purple Heart. Go get some chow. You and your teams report back here at 0800 hours."

At mess I sat with James and Lawrence. We talked about the night's events. The man who was killed was another of James' friends. "He was a good guy. Married, no kids. We met at the USO on my first day in country. He's from upstate New York, a town not far from home."

Lawrence noticed my arm and said, "Looks like you got nicked. You're collecting Purple Hearts, aren't you? You just got here and already you've been promoted and awarded two medals. I'm starting to think you're a show-off, Sergeant Baker." His joking always helped dispel the stress.

Back at the tent Smithson ordered me to divide the men into three teams, appoint a leader for each, and assign each team one of the three chores. Trucks were waiting to take the garbage team. The mess hall team was told to report to the officer-in-charge and sent on foot. The toilet maintenance team was marched to the camp maintenance shed for instructions. I was told to go with them to learn their duties. When they had been told what to do, they were issued shovels and taken away in trucks. I returned to first platoon's tent where Smithson was waiting.

We were the only ones there. The lieutenant had ordered me a small work desk. He handed over a clipboard and a stack of daily report forms, saying that the CO's were no longer confined to the tent.

He went on, "Baker, I was told you responded when the call for a medic came. You probably saved one man's life. You may be a CO, but you're not a coward. If you need anything, say so." I couldn't think what to say, but did realize he intended to convey respect and admiration. He turned to walk away. Finally, I came out with, "Thank you!" He didn't look back or reply.

All that morning, while the teams were doing their work, I updated the journal with the Guardians' words and the events of the night fight. That afternoon I wrote Karen a long letter about how much I missed home, and her.

The teams returned when their duties were done. All three were finished before evening chow. And, by all reports, the first day went smoothly. When they arrived, I relayed the order that we were no longer confined to the tent and sent them to the showers. After eating we went en masse to the USO for ice cream. When we arrived, "Strawberry Fields" was playing.

Chapter 17

ARREST

At 0800 the next morning all CO applicants reported to company headquarters to appear before boards of inquiry. Three boards had been convened because of the number of applicants.

Since my work teams were all CO applicants, I had no one to send out on trash, mess, or latrine duty. Lieutenant Smithson ordered me to remain at my desk, to wait for the applicants to return and then send them out.

About 0900 the first ones returned. All had their applications approved. They were jubilant. I was told that eleven more from our company had decided to apply, bringing the total to fifty-five. All morning they trickled in. When enough had arrived to comprise a work team, I sent them out. By noon everyone had returned. I was told that all but one had been approved for CO status. I assigned the fifty-four to the remaining duties and told them to go straight to the showers when their work was finished.

That afternoon, while they were working, I filled out daily reports for that day and the day before, then took them to the company clerk. As I was leaving the first sergeant walked in and said, "Hold on Baker." He went to his desk, picked up a box with a Purple Heart inside and handed it to me. "I thought we agreed you wouldn't get another one."

"Sorry, First Sergeant. Nurse's instinct."

"That instinct is going to get you a Bronze Star too. Lieutenant Smithson put you in for it. But that's the last Purple Heart. Understood?" He looked me in the eye and smiled.

"Thanks, First Sergeant." It then occurred to me that an expected rebuke, for being at the center of the CO rebellion, wasn't going to happen. Apparently, Captain Stone was not going to punish me or the other CO's in his company beyond putting us on dirt duty. Evidently there was a growing recognition in the ranks that the war was not going to be won. Maybe those in charge were feeling more sympathetic toward the men who had to put their lives on the line for a lost cause. Giving out medals was one way of showing that sympathy.

Things continued to go smoothly for the next three weeks. I opted to rotate duties so no one had to do the same job every day. None of the jobs were enviable but working in the mess hall was definitely preferred. Some days I would go out to assist one team or another. Other days I would stay at my desk doing paperwork and writing in the journal.

One day, I decided to ride along with the garbage team. There were three of us in the cab of the truck, and two riding in the back. As we drove out of the truck shed, the man between me and the driver took a small pipe out of his shirt pocket and said, "Care for a pull?" He lit the pipe and passed it to me.

"What is it," I asked.

"Opium and hash," he replied. "Makes the work a little more agreeable."

"Better not," I said. "You guys could get an Article Fifteen for that, maybe even a court-martial. And the CO's could get a bad rap."

They sensed my disapproval. The man put the pipe back in his pocket and no more was said. I wondered how many other CO's were partaking. I knew if the officers found out, there would be trouble.

Three days later, in the morning, after the men had been sent out, the lieutenant and the first sergeant showed up at my desk. They looked displeased. Smithson said, "Baker, we got a report that there's dope smoking in your group. Know anything about it?"

"Sir, I do know about one incident. I let the men know I didn't approve."

The first sergeant asked, "Do you have any, Baker?"

"No, First Sergeant."

"We have to do a search," he said. "Take off your fatigues." I thought about protesting, then decided not to, and stripped down to green tee shirt and boxers.

They went through the fatigue pockets and found nothing incriminating. Smithson pulled my duffel bag from underneath my bunk and dumped the contents out. A long-stemmed opium pipe fell out with my personal gear and the bowl was stuffed with a brownish substance. He picked it up and sniffed the bowl. They both looked at me.

The lieutenant held it up and said, "What's this, Baker?"

I was dumbfounded. I looked at both of them and said, "That's not mine." They didn't appear inclined to believe me.

"You're under tent arrest, Sergeant Baker, pending an investigation. You can go to chow and the showers only," Smithson said. "A hearing will be convened. You will continue with your duties but you will remain here until you receive further orders. If you're caught smoking or more evidence turns up, you will be put in the base stockade. Understood?"

I began to shake my head in disbelief but military protocol kicked in. Realizing how bad this was—and how serious the officers were—I managed to weakly reply, "Yes, sir."

I knew someone had put the pipe in my duffel, but who? I didn't think any of the objectors would set me up like that. I didn't say anything to anyone. Apparently, neither did the lieutenant. Two days went by. I received no orders to report for a hearing. The longer I waited the more I longed to confer with Joyah and Rayah. But they didn't appear. On the third day, when the men were out and I was alone in the tent, I began thinking about my Guardians' advice to devote time to prayer and worship, and how I had not fulfilled my promise to incorporate them into daily life. I decided to try praying.

I sat with elbows on my desk, hands clasped together, then closed my eyes. I wondered how to begin. It occurred that I might ask who had planted the pipe in my belongings. But then I felt that wasn't the right thing to ask. Another moment went by and I recalled something Joyah had said about praying—to ask for values, not things.

I cleared my mind and began anew, this time asking for wisdom, patience, courage, and understanding. Suddenly I had a feeling of lightness. No words came to mind, but there was an unmistakable assurance that everything would turn out for the best. I opened my eyes and the assurance I sensed remained.

Then I thought about the Guardians' encouragement to worship. I closed my eyes again and asked how to do it; how does one enter worship? No sooner had I asked than a feeling of being embraced by a powerful love unfolded. It was also a feeling of unity, being one with all. It was stronger, even more pleasurable and encompassing than the hugs with Rayah and Joyah. How long it lasted I'm not sure, but I've never forgotten it. And many times after that I've sought this embrace. It somehow dispels any and all fears. And more than that, creativity is enhanced. It's remarkable really.

Chapter 18

CONFESSION

That night, not long after lights-out, a series of tremendous explosions shook the ground. The shock waves blew our tent around until it seemed it might collapse. We ran for shelter in the bunker next to our tent. I brought the medic's pouch this time. The string of explosions lasted for almost a minute, followed by isolated ones. We could hear yelling and screaming coming mostly from the direction of the base arsenal.

James yelled over the noise, "Mortars must have hit the ammo dump." We could hear a man nearby, screaming for help. He staggered into our bunker. I recognized his wounds. He had been hit with white phosphorous.

Bits of phosphorous were burning into the man's flesh all along his right side, from head to toe. He was panicked and agonizing as the chemical bored ever deeper into skin and muscle.

I knew phosphorous will keep burning as long as it is exposed to the air. I grabbed a canteen that was sitting on a shelf and poured water onto the ground, then stirred it with my fingers making mud. I made him lie down on his left side, "Hold him, and help me put mud on each burn." Two men held him and two others followed my lead, dipping their hands in the mud and smearing it in the wounds. "Somebody call an ambulance," I yelled. James made the call over the bunker's walkie-talkie. There were dozens of punctures where the phosphorous had penetrated. Almost all of his right side was covered with mud by the time we had finished. He was still writhing in pain. I gave him an injection of morphine.

After a few minutes, he calmed down enough to talk. "Oh man, it burns. I'm going to be messed up for life, aren't I?" He began sobbing. "Why did this happen? I was going home in three months."

I shined a light on his nametag. "You're going to be all right, Jones," I said. "An ambulance has been called."

Then we heard over the radio, "Hold on Bunker 56, there are a lot of calls. We'll get to you when we can."

"Oh, damn, hurry!" Jones cried out. I gave him another dose of morphine, took out my ink pen and wrote "M+2" on his forehead and his left arm.

I asked him questions to distract from the pain; it looked like he was going into shock. "Where you from, Jones?"

"Walla-Walla. Am I going to make it home? Oh God, I can't die like this. I was just leaving guard duty at the ammo dump when I heard mortars coming in. White phosphorous grenades went off everywhere!"

"Take it easy. We're going to get you fixed up," I assured him. But I wasn't that sure myself. I learned in school that shock can kill a person, especially in combination with wounds like his. "What company are you with?"

"Company A, fourth platoon. I was going to my bunk when I was hit."

The morphine was starting to do its job and he wasn't in as much pain. "I'm Baker, Company A, first platoon. Call me, Ernie. How about some water?" He took a big drink from the canteen.

"Baker? You're the CO, aren't you?"

James said, "That's him."

Suddenly Jones turned pale. His pulse got rapid and unsteady. Shock was setting in. "Hang in there, Jones," I said. "The ambulance is on the way."

In spite of my assurances he sensed his life might be slipping away. His voice was weak but calm. He reached out and took hold of my shirt. "Ernie. I wish I was a CO. Maybe this wouldn't have happened. Listen, there's something I should tell

111

you. There's this guy in my platoon... he doesn't like CO's. He thinks you're all cowards and traitors. He told some of us he was going to fix you guys. He went into the village and bought a pipe and some opium. He said he was going to put it in your things and then report it to the first sergeant. I didn't think it was right. I should have said something. I'm sorry."

James said, "Who was it, Jones?"

"A guy they call Wicky. He's got a long name nobody can pronounce. It wasn't right, what he did. I didn't like it, but I didn't want to stir up more trouble. I wish I had said something. I was afraid he might do something to me. I'm really sorry."

The radio crackled on, "It'll be at least a half hour, Bunker 56." James acknowledged it.

Then Jones whispered, "If I don't make it, will you write to my wife, Mary? Tell her I love her. Tell her I'll see her on the other side of the river. She'll know what that means."

"Hold on. You're going to make it. You can write her yourself." I looked at Lawrence and James and asked, "Is there a jeep or a truck so we can get him to the hospital?"

James went out and came back in saying, "The jeep is burned. Could we carry him on cot?"

"We could, if we had several men to help," I said. Everyone in the bunker volunteered. Just then Jones coughed and slumped. I checked for a pulse. Nothing. I looked at his pupils. They were wide open.

I pulled his wallet out of his pants pocket. There was a picture of him and a young woman. On the back it was written, "Love you, see you in 365 days, Mary." I copied his home address from his driver's license.

All the explosions had stopped. Little fires were burning everywhere outside our bunker. It wasn't long before Lieutenant Smithson arrived. He wrote down Jones' serial number, then said, "Baker, take the CO's to the hospital and pitch in wherever you're needed. Double time."

We ran, in ragged formation, the two kilometers to the base hospital. It was hellish until we got away from the area around the ammo dump. The scene at the hospital was chaotic. An officer with a Red Cross armband met us and sent us to the triage area. The rest of the night and into the morning we carried wounded men on stretchers to and from the wards. Many of them had phosphorous burns, and some also had shrapnel wounds. Not all survived. We loaded several bodies onto an ambulance for transport to the base morgue.

When everyone was treated we were released to return to our unit. Exhaustion was setting in, along with the emotional toll of battle and blood. We slowly walked back to our bunks and crashed for the rest of the day. Most of us woke in time for evening chow. It was a meager meal. The mess hall was understaffed.

When we had finished eating, James and Lawrence went to the officer's table and asked to speak to our lieutenant. They walked a short distance and began conversing. I saw James pointing to a man. They all three went to talk to him. The lieutenant led the man outside. They were followed by four other men. Lawrence and James came back to our table.

They sat down and James said, "That was Wicky. Four from his squad confirmed what Jones told you last night. You're in the clear, Ernie. Why didn't you tell us you'd been framed?"

Lawrence joked, "Yeah, Sergeant Baker, you could have told us. We would have informed the lieutenant that you only deal opium on weekends."

We could see the lieutenant outside the mess hall listening to Wicky's protests. After a few minutes MP's came and took him away. He glared at us as they walked him to a jeep and then drove away with him in the back. We heard later that he was sent home with a dishonorable discharge.

After dinner, I went back to my bunk. Smithson was in the tent. He walked over and said, "You've been cleared, Baker.

You're no longer under tent arrest. And I have more good news. The army has decided to contract out garbage, mess, and latrine duties. Philippino work crews have been brought in. You and the other CO's have been reassigned to the base hospital. You'll still be in charge of the CO's. And you'll still bunk here. Understood?" He stuck out his hand for a shake.

Just before lights-out that night, when everyone was present, I made the announcement. A great cheer went up.

Chapter 19

HOSPITAL DUTY

Since I had no training as an administrator, Lieutenant Smithson suggested I appoint James and Lawrence to help manage the CO's. It was James who marched them to the hospital on that first morning. Lawrence and I took a jeep in order to arrive ahead of them. We reported to the hospital's commanding officer. She was a life-long army nurse with a big smile and a warm heart. It was obvious she was accustomed to handling responsibility. When her clerk introduced us, she stuck out her hand and gave a very firm handshake, saying, "Major Margaret Fisher. You can call me what everyone else does, Major Maggie, or better yet, just Maggie. So, you're in charge of Baker's Brigade, all CO's I hear. How many in your unit, Sergeant Baker?"

"Fifty-four, Ma'am. Please, call me Ernie."

"All right, Ernie. I'm glad you showed up. We need help around here, business is picking up. You and your men will be on-call. You'll work triage when the wounded arrive, carrying stretchers, assisting the doctors and nurses. When there's nothing else to do, you'll work the wards, fetching supplies, helping out, and cleaning as needed. You'll prep and take the fallen ones to the morgue, too. Understood?"

"Yes, Ma'am."

"It says here you're a nurse. Where'd you go to school?"

"University of Texas, Austin."

"Drafted out of school? No work experience?"

"No, Ma'am. Just ten months army training before coming to Nam, and a month OJT here."

"Your record says you got two Purple Hearts already, and you're up for a Bronze Star. Impressive, Sergeant. Good to have

115

you on board. When your men arrive, take them to the conference tent and give them an idea of what's expected of hospital aides. Divide them into two groups and schedule half for day shift and half for night. We work seven days a week here, no time off except for illness, leave, or R & R. Assign a leader for each shift, someone who shows talent for using, but not abusing, authority. You'll get chow at the hospital mess hall. If bunks are available your men can rest in the conference tent during their off time. I'll expect a daily report from you first thing every morning. Any questions?"

"No, Ma'am. Not now anyway."

She then said to her clerk, "Requisition a desk and chair. Set Sergeant Ernie up in the triage tent."

Then to me, "I should add, after you've divided your men into two shifts, divide each shift into three groups, one group for each of our three wards. Today you can dismiss the night shift and have them report for duty at midnight. The day shift can report at 1200 hours. All right?"

"Yes, Ma'am... Major Maggie."

"You'll do just fine, Ernie. But don't hesitate to bring any personnel problems to me. Dismissed." She ordered her clerk, "Show them to the conference tent."

James had already arrived with my little "brigade." They were standing at parade rest, waiting for instructions. I signaled them to follow. The clerk led us to the conference tent where I conveyed Maggie's instructions and gave them an outline of our duties. We were finished by 0930. I dismissed them and told the day shift to report for duty at noon, the night shift at midnight.

Since there was nothing to do until noon, Lawrence drove James and me to the USO for coffee. We discussed our new assignment. I suggested, "Why don't you two be the shift leaders? At least until we see who among our brigade shows signs of leadership."

Lawrence volunteered, "I'll take night shift, unless the Thane wishes to lead it."

James replied, "Day shift is fine with me. Working nights messes with my chemistry."

"I'm happy to be back at hospital work. But not sure I'm cut out to manage others doing it," I confessed.

Lawrence immediately said, "Not to worry, General Baker. Your brigade will shine like a beacon on a hill. How could you fail when we're at your side?" James and I laughed.

James patted me on the back. I thanked them both for their willing assistance and encouraged the giving of any advice they might offer as this assignment unfolded. After coffee, Lawrence drove us back to the hospital. He returned to the relative quiet of Smithson's tent, to rest up for night shift.

It seemed only right to be available at the beginning of each shift—especially on the first day—in order to train the CO's in hospital work. Carrying stretchers didn't take much training, but they needed to know whom to report to on the wards, how to help the nurses turn a patient, where to get supplies, and like duties. Before the day shift showed up, I divided their names into three groups, assigned each group to a ward, then did the same for the night shift. I asked James and Lawrence to do roll call at the beginning of each shift.

During the first few days it was gratifying to see how well the CO team adapted. No one complained about long hours, emptying bedpans, or changing bloody sheets. This was due mostly to the fact that hospital duty is much easier, and safer, than carrying a weighty pack on your back all day under the burning sun while being shot at. It was obvious all the CO's wanted to hang onto this duty for the rest of their tour. Therefore, they were easy to manage—obedient and willing workers.

For me the first days were stressful, simply because everything was new. But soon enough a routine was established and I became accustomed to playing supervisor. I would be there for each shift change. When everything was going smoothly I would retire for rest or deskwork. James and Lawrence proved to be excellent managers, handling most problems themselves and making sure all that needed doing was done in good time. On the first day, Ralph and Sammy were transferred to my command. Having already served at the hospital for a while, they proved to be very helpful in training the others.

The biggest event during the first weeks of hospital duty wasn't in Nam. It was at home, when Martin Luther King, Jr. was killed. King was a hero to millions of young people, regardless of ethnicity or skin tone. He was an unrelenting and vocal opponent of the Vietnam invasion besides being a spiritual icon. African-American men and women had a significant role in the war. Indeed, eighteen of the fifty-four CO's were men of color, and several of the nurses with whom we worked were of diverse racial origin.

King died one year after giving his famous sermon against the war, "Beyond Vietnam, A Time to Break Silence." I heard it over the radio just after having received a draft notice. I never forgot his stirring words decrying the use of napalm, our supporting the corrupt and autocratic government of South Vietnam, and the growing number of squandered lives of conscripts. His speech was a significant factor in my decision to become a Conscientious Objector. I was especially moved by his reference to the dangers of staying neutral and quiet in the face of wrong. Six weeks after that speech I was inducted into the army and put on a bus headed for training at Fort Sam Houston. Ten months later I landed in Vietnam.

At the hospital, we listened to the radio whenever we could, and passed around dated newspapers sent from home in order to keep abreast of the tumultuous aftermath of King's assassination. Race riots and fires rolled through the big cities of the US, severely singeing the fabric of American society. From what we heard and read, it seemed as if division and war was fracturing the homeland. It was depressing to think of America in such a state. I took refuge in the fact that the CO's remained united and friendly. African-American men weren't the only minorities in the CO group. There were Hispanics, Asians, and Native-Americans as well. Opposition to the war, even while being forced to participate in it, kept us united.

Chapter 20

A GRANDER VISION

Hospital duties kept the CO group busy day and night, me included. But never had I felt more useful and in service to my comrades, despite being witness to a gory parade. The stream of wounded and dead soldiers, arriving by helicopter and ambulance, was ceaseless. As 1968 unfolded, casualties on both sides increased. But so did the number of objectors. Every week several more CO's were added to our ranks. By June first there were seventy-seven.

On June 6, news of another high-profile event at home grabbed our attention. Robert Kennedy, a promising candidate for president and a formidable opponent of the war, was assassinated. I was saddened and disappointed, and knew that a great voice against the war had been silenced. Now it seemed inevitable that the conflict would go on, that even more men and money would be poured into the grinder of war. And so it did, for six more tragic years.

As other CO's joined our little brigade, and as the war expanded, more and greater needs were surfacing. I caught sleep whenever possible and had almost no time to write in the journal. I did make time to write home at least once a week, to mom and dad, and to Karen. Mom was good to send a "care package" every so often, stuffed with cookies, candies, family photos, newspaper articles, and current magazines.

No matter how busy it was, I always made time each day to go within, even if only for a few minutes. Praying and communing became anchors that tethered me to sanity in a place of madness. They also provided a beacon of optimism along with energy sufficient to meet the needs of the day. Seldom did I tire or feel depressed. And because it was so busy, time went quickly. In fact, it was a blur. During this period, I learned a great deal about administration and teamwork. James and Lawrence were matchless helpers, always taking charge when they should and asking for help when appropriate. And they never complained. Both confessed to feeling better about the war by contributing to healing rather than killing.

Three months passed before Rayah and Joyah visited again. It happened late one night after a rather rare, lax day. I was sleeping in a cot at the hospital's conference tent. Meeting them again was wonderfully refreshing and uplifting. I realized just how much I missed them.

After we embraced, Joyah held me at arm's length and said, "You have been making remarkable progress administering a large team. We are very pleased, Ernie. Successfully managing a working group to achieve good ends is a valuable skill, one you will find useful as you progress in your adventure of eternal life. You are doing so well, learning so much every day, that we thought it best not to disrupt what little rest you manage to get. Since you have an extended rest period tonight we would tell you more about the next-life rewards of faithful stewardship of this life. About the play and recreation that you will enjoy as you ascend the seven mansion worlds."

Rayah continued, "When you graduate to the mansion world career, you will discover there are two central activities: service and recreation. Your time there is about evenly divided between them. Smiles—and laughter—are universal on the mansion worlds, and so is music. Joy and mirth are inherent qualities of spiritual living. But all these things surpass your human versions. On the mansions you will encounter a group of beings whose service is to entertain, to use humor to uplift. Good humor has the ability to prevent destructive self-contemplation. Humor and play are divine remedies for too much seriousness. Just as new duties and new truths stretch a growing soul, so will humor and play quickly relieve accumulating tensions. A bit of laughter has the power to trigger the benefits of relaxation. Ernie, in heaven there is no anxiety as you now understand it."

Joyah added, "Your witty friend Lawrence might well be recruited as a member of the rotating group of celestial humorists. Good humor is a spiritual phenomenon; it creates joy and enhances the experience of living and learning. The negative humor of humans, on the other hand, creates cynicism and despair. Good humor never disparages the weak or the unfortunate, and never is it irreverent or mean-spirited. While negative humor is usually crude and offensive, good humor is always refreshing and energizing. Bad humor can be sarcastic and caustic; good humor is always respectful and thoughtful."

Rayah went on, "Being entertained by humorists is not the only form of recreation and diversion on high. For every manner and kind of amusement, pleasure, and merriment you have on Earth, there are thousands on the mansion spheres. You will find the equivalent of movies, books, and music, but many magnitudes greater. You will have the freedom and means to travel to places far beyond the range of your imagination. And these destinations are not limited to one sphere. There are other worlds far in advance, physically, culturally, and spiritually. The diversity of the activities and the array of pleasures would stagger your imagination—if you possessed the conceptual framework required to reveal them. It is better that you discover them one by one as you ascend to the ultimate sphere whereon the God of the universes abides. Mansion World Number One will seem like a paradise to you, but where the Universal Father dwells is the final Paradise. Ernie, have no doubt that one day you will arrive there."

These revelatory insights were very comforting. After pondering them a moment, I remarked, "From all you've told me, an expanded vision of heaven has been forming in my mind. During prayer and worship, sometimes I imagine life there… maybe because I see so much death here, and know it could take me any day. And too, I like knowing dying men are going to a better place. Because of that, I very much appreciate you giving these insights. They add to my overall vision, and that keeps away most of the fear of dying. While you were talking about recreation, I wondered if you have favorite activities. What do Guardian Angels enjoy doing?"

Joyah answered, "Since we have been in existence much longer than you, we have already explored all the mansion worlds, and many other worlds to which you will someday ascend. But it will be our great pleasure, while guiding your progress, to experience them again through your eyes. Just as a parent derives pleasure from a child's explorations and recreational activities, so do we Guardians derive vicarious enjoyment and service satisfaction from our mortal partners' worthwhile experiences in education and play. Our greatest pleasure, however, comes from divine worship. You will learn in time and through practice that worshipful communion transcends all other pleasures."

This encounter, and these lessons, made me realize there had been an evolution in my worship over the last months, from misunderstanding and trial to an enjoyable and sustaining experience. An experience without which I would now feel incomplete.

Chapter 21

BREAK-UP

During the next three months thirty-five more Conscientious Objectors joined the brigade. I was kept extremely busy welcoming, orienting, and training them. The flow of casualties was relentless as the Viet Cong and North Vietnamese armies staged several "mini-Tets," in order to keep pressure on the occupiers. The year 1968 recorded the highest number of wounded and killed, on both sides of the Vietnam war.

Mom and dad could be depended on for family news, to send packages of homemade desserts, requested snacks, and personal needs. But letters from Karen became less and less frequent, and with diminishing intimacy. The feeling that she might be dating another was confirmed by a letter received on my sixth-month anniversary in Nam.

After several weeks of not hearing from her, I wrote to ask about it. She replied right away. Her words conveyed a beautiful sentiment so characteristic of her. She expressed deep sorrow on having to inform me that she wished to end our courtship. I know it hurt her almost as much as it did me. She went on to say that she and Mike Manning, a fellow art student, someone I knew, had been dating. He was a good artist, also a pilot. He had taken Karen up and proposed to her as they flew around the city of Austin. They planned to marry on Christmas Eve.

The army tries to prepare its soldiers for the likelihood that their lovers and mates might leave them while they are away. Many times during basic training, we would sing cadence while jogging in formation. One song was about a man named Jody, a fictitious rascal who steals your lover's heart as you serve your country. The song contained a repeating line, "Jody's got her now."

Karen's letter hit hard, but it wasn't unexpected. It made me realize no relationship with another human is beyond dissolution. And it had an added benefit, that of strengthening my spiritual connection. After receiving her letter, I went to a small chapel that was adjacent to the USO café. There, all alone, I had an especially intimate moment of inner communion. I wept a bit, but came away with a more mature perspective, one that served me well in those days and since.

Not long after Karen's "Dear John letter," Maggie sent word that, in two weeks, I was scheduled for five days "Rest and Recreation." R & R is a sort of vacation that all who serve in Nam were afforded. We had a choice of travel to several locations, even Hawaii. Also offered were Sydney, Singapore, Taipei, Bangkok, Kuala Lampur, Hong Kong, and Manila.

When Lawrence and James heard, we decided to request going together. Maggie approved it on the condition that we find responsible and well-trained men to take our places, which we did. After several days of hearing reports from those who had been on R & R, we decided to go to Bangkok. It wasn't my first choice, but it was theirs. I thought Sydney might be the most interesting. But anywhere that didn't have a war suited me.

It was a short flight, on a commercial airline, to the capital of Thailand. There was a full planeload, about two hundred men. On arrival we were marched to an orientation room. An intimidating-looking sergeant major stood at the front of the room and delivered a canned speech.

"Welcome to Bangkok, men. You will be here for five days, and no longer. If you stay longer, you will be reported as absent without leave. Anyone who goes AWOL will receive an Article Fifteen. While you are here you will obey army rules and observe local customs. The US Army is a guest of the Thai government and any offense you commit while you are here will reflect on the US Army. At no point during your visit to this country will you exhibit any PDA, a public display of affection. The women you will fraternize with all have health cards. If you fraternize with a woman who does not have such a card and you contract 'a cold,' you will receive an Article Fifteen. The prices for card-carrying women are the same everywhere: eleven dollars per twelve hours. If you abuse, misuse, or otherwise harm these women you will receive an Article Fifteen, or be court-martialed. Drunken behavior will not be tolerated. It will result in immediate termination of your R & R. Is that understood? Any questions?"

Even though we had heard much about Bangkok R & R before arriving, I was astonished by the frank and open, army sanctioned and managed, sex trade. But I understood the army was protecting its own interests by first, providing relief from pent up sex hunger and the longing for female attention, restrained as they are by the business of war and months of service in a nearly all-male environment. And second, making sure soldiers didn't return to duty with venereal diseases.

After orientation, the first thing we did was pick a taxi driver. They were lined up outside waiting for us to emerge. We chose an amiable fellow named Mr. Po. His English was passable and his experience long. He recommended we first get a room and then go out on the town for a meal. Mr. Po got us a "special rate" at the Hotel Bangkok, a thirty-story building with many bars nearby, bars that catered to visiting soldiers' needs. We each got a room, dropped off our duffel bags, and rejoined Mr. Po for a ride to a restaurant, also having "a special rate," no doubt a kickback for Mr. Po. The seafood was delicious, along with an ice-cold, quart-size, bottle of Singha beer.

After lunch we went for a stroll. It was a beautiful day. It caused Lawrence to wax poetic, "O sweet life, how I adore walking down a war-less street, breathing air where no helicopter doth fly. And reveling in a place where nary a weapon may be seen nor heard."

It felt very liberating to be at a place of peace, the burden of perpetual angst temporarily lifted. Living in a war zone carries with it an underlying feeling of conflict, anxiety, and turmoil. Even though the war was but a few hundred miles away, Bangkok felt like it could be on another planet. It was a busy metropolis with every form of transportation, from cart-drawn horses to air conditioned buses, and all driving on the left side. Lawrence was fascinated by this and begged Mr. Po to let him drive. He took us to a relatively quiet city street and let Lawrence have the wheel for a ride around the block only. Lawrence grinned like a kid on a new bike, and didn't make any mistakes except to confuse the brake with the clutch once.

After that Mr. Po took us on a tour of the city's most visited tourist spots, including the King's palace and the floating market. We went to a jewelry shop, another place with special rates for friends of Mr. Po. There we bought fine wristwatches for ourselves, sapphire rings and sparkling trinkets as gifts for moms and sisters. James purchased a Nikon 35mm camera that he wanted to take to the post office and ship straight home, fearing Vietnam's humidity might damage it. While at the post office, I visited the public restroom. It consisted of a series of large holes in the floor with footpads on each side of the hole. While I urinated in one, an old woman entered and without the least hesitation or concern, raised her dress and squatted over one of the holes. I held the door for her as we exited.

Back at the hotel we showered, shaved, and dressed in civilian clothes for an evening out. Mr. Po asked to be released to go home for the night. He arranged to meet us the next morning for a motor tour of the countryside. Before departing he suggested in broken English that we, "Get dinner at hotel, then go to bars, get girl, all near to hotel." The hotel had a first-rate restaurant located on one side of its inner courtyard. We opted to dine outdoors, by the pool, ordering cheeseburgers and fries, a house specialty. It was a taste of home.

Chapter 22

PORTIA

Nightclubs lined the street adjacent to Hotel Bangkok. All had flashing neon signs, depicting alluring dancing girls, enticing the soldier to enter. GI's were everywhere, their "white sidewall" haircuts, shorts, and flowery shirts giving them away. Most were with a young, attractive, Asian woman. Some were with two. Money was not an issue. We'd been sitting on our pay for months, with few places to spend it in Nam.

We surveyed the territory and finally decided on one of the nicer clubs. Pulsing music animated dozens of young women on the dance floor. Very few men were dancing. It became evident the women were on display, showing their wares. The tables were occupied by partying GI's.

We took a seat, ordered drinks, and watched. Before long we realized how things worked. When a man decided which woman he wished to hire for the night he would signal a waiter. The waiter would come to the table, the man would indicate which dancer, and the waiter would shine a flashlight on her. She would then come to the table for a drink and a financial arrangement.

While popular songs played—by James Brown, the Beatles, Simon and Garfunkel, and others—the drinks kept coming. And as the night descended outside, jubilation reached a fever pitch inside. Inhibitions quickly waned, replaced by a longing for companionship. We watched as one girl after another was selected. Before long, James and Lawrence summoned the waiter to shine a light on their choices. All I could think about was the girls. Did these young women really want to be here? What do their parents think? And how did they come to be prostitutes?

The two girls that James and Lawrence selected seemed to be enjoying themselves, sitting at our table laughing and joking. Both were about eighteen or nineteen, and spoke

128

understandable English. They asked our names and gave their adopted western names, Tina and Linda.

They teased me. Linda kept asking, "Don't you like girls?" and "Are you shy?" Finally Tina said, "We get you girl. What kind you like?" James suggested a nurse.

"We know nurse!" Tina exclaimed and called the waiter. She pointed to a twenty-something looking woman. The waiter shined the light and she came to the table. Linda introduced us, "Ernie, this my friend Portia." She sat next to me, smiling just a bit, glancing at my face then looking away. She didn't seem embarrassed, but was more restrained and reserved than Linda and Tina.

She had a lovely face, and a knowing look in her eye. She may have been young but didn't in the least appear to be naïve.

Lawrence finished his drink and suggested, "Let's go for a stroll." We paid our bar bill and the waiter explained that we should also pay him the eleven-dollar fee for the girls.

The balmy night air was invigorating after being in the smoky club. The streets were lined with couples and groups like ours, with lots of laughter and loud talk. We walked several blocks until arriving at a relatively quiet park. It had many benches amid short trees heavy with flowering vines. Lawrence and James took a seat on one bench. Portia and I kept walking. She took my hand in hers.

"You're a nurse?" I asked.

"Yes, soon. I take classes."

"At a university?"

"Yes, medical school."

"Where will you work when you graduate?"

"I will go to my home, near Chiang Mai." It was obvious she was educated. She had much less accent than either Tina or Linda.

"You have family there?"

"No family," she replied with a wisp of sadness.

We found an empty bench and sat. Nothing was said. A full moon was directly overhead. It was comforting to be in the presence of a woman. At the same time, I wondered if she really wanted to be there with me. Surely an aspiring nurse would prefer to be working anywhere other than a Bangkok bar that services soldiers.

"Is Portia your given name?"

"It's my work name. My real name is Mailee."

"Why Portia?"

"You know Shakespeare? I like his plays."

"As I recall from English class, Portia is a beautiful, witty, woman who persuades Shylock to be merciful with his borrowers."

"Yes, she is strong and smart. She cares for people. I care for people too."

"That's why you're a nursing student?"

"Yes. I don't like working at bar."

"Why do you?"

"No other jobs for woman, except very low pay. This way I get enough money for nursing school."

"Where are your parents, your family?"

"They die. No sisters or brothers. One aunt in Chiang Mai. Very old."

After a few minutes more, simply absorbing the moment, we stood and slowly walked hand in hand toward James, Lawrence, Tina, and Linda. As we approached they were caressing, talking softly, and laughing.

James said, "Let's head over to the hotel." Back on the

lighted street we refrained from any PDA. Nightlife was in full swing. Music was blasting out of every club door. Soldiers in civvies, primed with alcohol, were everywhere. Almost all were in the company of friends, each with a Thai girl.

Lawrence and James retired to their rooms with Tina and Linda. I invited Portia to have coffee. We took a table by the pool and ordered a pastry to go with coffee.

Portia asked, "You have a girlfriend at home?"

"No. No more."

"She leave you?"

"Yes, I got a letter saying she's marrying someone else."

"Sorry."

"It's OK. How about you?"

"No boyfriend. In Thailand, no man wants bar girl."

"You don't like it, do you?"

"No, I wish not to be."

"How long until you have your nursing license?"

"One year, about. You have license, already?"

"I do. As soon as I left school, the army called. Now I work at a hospital in Chu Lai, Vietnam, for six more months. Then back home."

"You like Vietnam?"

"I don't like the war. But I am learning a lot about how to treat wounds and save lives."

"I hate war. Why do men do it? Thailand fights in Laos now, to help America. We have Air Force base for America."

"War is something humans can't seem to avoid. Maybe, someday, we will realize there are better ways to solve our problems. But then the world won't need as many nurses!" She laughed for the first time. It was a joy to hear.

"How is it you know Shakespeare? Where did you learn about Portia?"

"Before my parents die, I was in good school. Parents were teachers there. We learned English and performed plays from Shakespeare in English and Thai. I like his words."

"How did they die?"

"Car crash. I miss them very much. They love me. But when they die, all money go to expenses."

I reached across the table and took her hands. She seemed to appreciate it. We looked each other in the eye. It was a moment of human connection and understanding.

"Portia… Mailee, I don't want sex. But, will you spend the night with me?" She looked at me and nodded.

We went to my room and stayed up several hours talking about family, friends, politics, everything, until the caffeine wore off. She had a broad knowledge of the world and a wise philosophy of living. Her background was Buddhist but she and I shared the same basic beliefs about the meaning, purpose, and value of life. And that there had to be a God to create such an infinite, complex, and personal universe.

When it was time to rest, we shed our outer layers and laid down. We drew near and cuddled. The intimacy of it filled me. I thought of Karen, now cuddling with Mike.

For the remainder of R & R, Portia and I stayed together. One day she showed me her rented room. It was tiny, with only a foam mattress on the floor, a small dresser, mirror, and a storage closet. Many others lived in the building, in similar quarters. She shared a bathroom with ten other women in the sex trade.

Our time together was gentle and caring, something we needed and gladly drank in. We had both suffered loss. She, an only child, had recently lost her parents. And I had just lost Karen's love. We didn't need to fill every minute with talk, just being together was enough. That both of us were nurses helped, but there was also a feeling of kindred-ness. On our first morning, well before sunrise, I awoke to Portia tugging my arm, saying gently, "Wake up. Let's walk...to a place I know."

We showered, dressed, and took the elevator to the lobby. She led me out the rear entrance. There were fireflies everywhere, it was magical. Not far down a well beaten and dimly lit path we came to the city's central river. The boats that served as floating shops during the day still had on their night covers. It was quiet for a city center, only an occasional, distant honk, a French siren, or a dog bark.

"I come here some mornings and sit," she whispered. We walked up to wooden bench. Portia brushed off the fallen leaves, took a seat and invited me to join her.

"You like this quiet?" she asked.

"Amazing, here in the city's center." I replied.

"You wait."

She closed her eyes and took several slow deep breaths. I did the same. Then we just listened. My thinking ceased and I became intensely aware of every sound. I began to feel like part of the environment. It must have lasted several minutes. Then, the loudest rooster I've ever heard sang out, announcing the new day. Instantly, several others chimed in. In a few seconds, there must have been hundreds crowing at the very top of their lungs from every boat and house on the river, seemingly trying to outdo the others. It was all but deafening.

My eyes popped open, she was watching me, we both burst out laughing. Portia really enjoyed playing this little mediation trick on me. And I never forgot the feeling of oneness, or the rousing rooster roar that made us laugh so good.

Lawrence and James hired a different girl each night and dismissed them at daybreak. We three and Portia palled around during the day, going on daily excursions in Mr. Po's taxi. We came to appreciate Thai culture and its ancient ways. Mr. Po took us to several restaurants outside the city, places GI's didn't frequent. He and Portia would order for us. No matter what was ordered, it was spicy hot. Portia laughed as we broke out in a sweat and shed tears. The fiery food didn't faze her or Mr. Po.

It was a joy to travel Thailand's peaceful countryside. The natural beauty of the land and the vegetation fascinated me. Thailand has a diverse climate, with highlands in the north. Vast rice paddies dominate the lowlands. I learned it was called Siam until 1939. Thailand was never colonized like many Asian nations, because it played France against Britain. It was forced to cooperate with Japan in World War II. In 1968, Thailand was a de facto American province, bringing in money from army tourists and military bases.

Portia and I thoroughly enjoyed our time together. No doubt these few days were a refreshing break for her, not having to compete for customers, not being compelled to provide them with sex pleasures. I treasured having her company, as opposed to participating in the insanity of war every hour of every day.

When the time came to leave, we said good-bye in front of the hotel. She and I exchanged addresses and promised to write. We pledged eternal friendship, and shared a long and satisfying hug. We simply forgot PDA. She waved goodbye to Lawrence, James, and me, as Mr. Po entered the traffic stream and ferried us to the airport. On the flight back I worked on a written record of the trip.

Chapter 23

A MISSION

Facing the war again after five days away in a comparative paradise was a bit depressing. Before reporting for duty, Lawrence, James, and I visited the USO for burgers and ice cream.

Lawrence tried to lighten the mood. "Well gentlemen, we're getting shorter by the minute. James and I will be in country just 121 days and 119 days more, respectively. Let's see, General Ernie... you have 180 days left to serve here in Shangri-la by the South China Sea?"

"Something like that," I replied.

James said, "Looks like we might make it home in one piece. I don't relish the idea of going back to work at the hospital, seeing so many men mangled and dead, but we most definitely have it better than some. I wish we would be the last ones to leave Nam."

"Fat chance, Thane! Leaving now would wound Uncle Sam's pride and send a message of surrender to Uncle Mao. It's important that both sides continue maiming and killing, in the name of peace of course," Lawrence replied with a cynical half-smile.

We hitched a ride to first platoon's tent, stowed our duffels, and reported our arrival to Lieutenant Smithson who ordered us back to hospital duty. Lawrence went for a jeep at the motor pool, then returned and drove us to the hospital where we reported to Maggie.

"Welcome back!" she said with a big and knowing smile. "You are sufficiently rested and relaxed I presume. Good! Because I have a mission for you. One of you anyway. Who wants to volunteer?"

Lawrence answered, "If you need someone to go to Hawaii for supplies, then I do indeed volunteer."

"Not quite that far. HQ issued orders to set up an aid station at a new landing zone in the boonies, a Marine base. LZ Amy by name. You'll need to take supplies, organize it, and wait to be replaced by a Navy corpsman who is on the way. Shouldn't take more than a week, but you may also have to treat wounded and sick until the corpsman arrives."

James said, "I'll go."

Lawrence said, "James is shorter than me. I'd better take this."

Maggie looked at me and said, "Actually, Ernie is the most qualified."

"It's settled then," I said. "When do I leave?"

She answered, "First thing tomorrow. I'll have a medivac bird, with all the supplies on board, ready and loaded by 0700."

Lawrence and James took charge of things at the hospital, giving me the day and night off. That afternoon and evening was spent updating my journal, making a copy to send home, along with a letter to mom and dad. I told them about R & R in Thailand; about making friends with Mailee. I mentioned going on a mission to set up a medical station for the Marines at LZ Amy. And I sent Mailee a thank you letter, including fifty dollars to help with her school fees.

That night I slept in my bunk in first platoon's tent. Joyah and Rayah paid a visit. After greeting me with a warm hug, Joyah said, "We were touched by your encounter with Mailee. And while you enjoyed each other's company, we came to know her Guardians. They were created at the same time we were, but that was the first crossing of our paths."

"I never thought to ask if she's talked with her angels. I'll have to remember that others have Guardians too. Are hers in contact, like you are with me?"

Rayah replied, "No, not yet. But Mailee's Guardians do expect great things. Her potential is estimated to be well above average. Her Guardians informed us that the time you spent together bolstered her determination to finish school and find better employment. And now she is thinking beyond nursing, she is contemplating becoming a doctor."

Joyah said, "You know Ernie, some of the most valuable lessons in life come out of hardship. Both you and Mailee are passing through what might be the most difficult experiences of your lives. These experiences are, in actuality, fiery furnaces that can temper the soft metal of immaturity into the hard steel of great character. Difficulties may defeat the timid and fearful, but they can also invigorate and stimulate a genuine truth-seeker. From the divine perspective there are no accidents, no unforeseen events. Every trying event can be used to advance the spiritual status of an aspiring mortal. Every effort may not produce joy, but without effort there can be no progress and no happiness. Remember always that righteous action results in augmented strength; that the weak make resolutions, but the strong act."

Rayah continued in the same vein, "We would have you realize that the worst of all afflictions is no affliction at all. Conflict and tribulation are designed to bring out the best, and to eliminate the worst. Stagnation is equivalent to bankruptcy in the spiritual economy. Spiritual truth is best discerned in adversity. But worry and anxiety must be avoided. Never forget that the soul is enriched not by what it does, but what it strives to do. God measures mortals by intention, not by accomplishment. What you choose to do today determines tomorrow's destiny. Greatness comes not from great strength but from good and wise use of available strength."

Joyah added, "There are certain inevitabilities inherent in planetary life. If you are to gain strength of character there must be hardship. If altruism is to manifest, there has to be inequality. If there is to be hope then there must exist uncertainty and insecurity. If faith is to spring to life then doubt must be an alternative. If truth is to be found and embraced then falseness must exist and be rejected. If divine idealism is to be instilled then mediocrity has to be present as a counterpoise. If loyalty is desired then the possibility of betrayal has to be available. If selflessness is to be part of well-balanced character, then the choice of selfishness has to be a factor. And if pleasure and enjoyment are to be had, pain and suffering must also be a possibility."

Rayah concluded by saying, "Ernie, we are not advocating that you seek out suffering and pain. We are saying that a certain amount of trouble and difficulty are inevitable in every life... that a life without affliction is a life not worth living. Health, wealth, and success can be enjoyed but clinging to them will only bring sorrow and pain. If a person lives long enough, health will deteriorate. Wealth may make you happy in the short-term, but it cannot bring long-term happiness. Successes may foster pride of accomplishment, but greater gains will be achieved by overcoming failure, and integrating the hard lessons wrought from disappointment. Much trouble and anxiety can be avoided by wise choosing. But wisdom is usually born of difficult experience and taking responsibility for such experience—not casting blame. Peace that passes understanding is born of alignment with divine ideals. Knowing, loving, and trusting God brings peace in circumstances both easy and difficult."

All this angelic advice was entered in the journal early the next morning. As I was writing, Lieutenant Smithson came by to give me a jewelry case containing a Bronze Star. He said nothing when I opened it, but gave a tight-lipped smile and stuck out his hand. We shook, he then turned and walked away.

I finished writing, stowed the medal in my duffel, packed a small zippered bag with personal items, went out on the roadway and hitched a ride to the hospital's heliport. While waiting for the chopper to be loaded I thought much about the role of difficulty and suffering in life. War certainly made both abundant. It provided an endless array of experiences that would be hard to forget. I was realizing just how much involvement in war changed people for the rest of their lives. I wondered how many were changed for the good, in the final analysis.

As I drifted in thought, the pilot jogged over and said, "We're loaded and ready, Sergeant Baker." There was just enough room for me and the medical supplies in the door-less cargo bay. It was packed full. There were no machine guns or gunners on board, just the pilot, the co-pilot, and me. The bird had large red crosses inside white circles painted on the fuselage and tail. It labored to lift off with the heavy load.

Chapter 24

CAPTURE

"Flight time is about twenty minutes," the co-pilot shouted as we departed basecamp. "Hang on tight."

There wasn't much room and the jump seats had supplies stacked on them too, so I was having a stand-up ride—and it was exhilarating. We flew close to the ground in order to minimize the risk of enemy gunfire and rocket-propelled grenades; the terrain was whizzing by beneath me. I enjoyed the rush of wind and speed, standing there in the cargo bay door holding fast to a hand strap.

About ten minutes into the flight we left the coastal flatlands and rice paddies behind and entered the foothills of the mountains. They were covered with thick jungle. Soon we were cruising just above the treetops as the pilots skillfully matched our flight path to the topography.

I could faintly hear the pilot communicating with someone over the radio. The co-pilot glanced back at me and hollered, "Eight minutes to LZ Amy." I nodded and gave him a thumbs-up. Then I heard and felt a BAAAMMM. Suddenly the helicopter lurched toward the jungle canopy. Flying so low, we quickly lost forward momentum and crashed into the trees, which threw me hard into the bird's metal frame and injured my shoulder. When all forward momentum stopped we began falling through the canopy. Huge tree limbs soon snared the bird but the unsecured supplies, along with me, poured out of the left side of the cargo bay. I could hear branches breaking and vines snapping as I and the supplies fell. The breath was knocked out of me on landing. It took a minute to recover.

Everything got still. I was lying on boxes and undergrowth that had cushioned my fall. Dazed but relieved to be alive with no serious injuries, I took several deep breaths and thanked God. Next I surveyed the surrounding jungle and looked up at the chopper hanging in the trees. The plexiglass cockpit was all but gone and still smoldering; that was where we took the hit. I didn't think the pilots could have survived and didn't see them. Then I heard a groan. The co-pilot was twenty feet away tangled in jungle brush and flailing his arm. I climbed off the boxes and ran to him. My left shoulder didn't feel broken but it was badly bruised and hurting.

He had sustained major injuries. He was bleeding badly from a neck wound and compound fractures of both legs. It was obvious, his death was imminent. "Mother?" That's all he said looking into the distance. In a brief moment he was gone.

Then I spotted the pilot several feet away in a tangle of leafy brush. He was ashen and broken, undoubtedly dead. As my own trauma and shock were setting in I sat there wondering what to do. My mind was racing with lots of scenarios, none of them good. Two comrades were dead and I was in no-man's land; there was little chance of rescue, and no radio to call for help.

Next, I heard voices and the sound of machetes hacking away at the jungle. They were speaking Vietnamese and they were coming close. I moved away and hid behind a large tree trunk. I could hear them talking as they arrived at the site. I peeked and saw that they were surveying the supplies. Suddenly, from behind, three men appeared and began yelling something at me. They came closer; one prodded me with his rifle muzzle, indicating that I should move toward the others. I put my hands up and complied.

When the others saw us, they approached and surrounded us. One was laughing and talking loudly, most likely boasting at downing a helicopter and capturing an enemy along with a load of medical supplies. "You, America!" he said with a heavy accent. I didn't say anything. I was shaking. I could tell shock was hitting my nervous system. The man reached for my dog tags and gave a jerk, breaking the chain. I assumed he must be in charge. He put the tags in his shirt pocket, then pushed me down and said something to one of his subordinates. That man kicked me until I rolled over onto my stomach. He tied my hands behind my back.

The leader barked out more orders. Two men stood me up; I let out an involuntary yelp because of the shoulder wound. Then they all picked up the boxes and we marched single file on the path they had hacked out to locate the crash site. There was a lot of chatter and laughter as we marched. After about a kilometer we came to a well-camouflaged encampment. We were met by dozens of cheering men and women. They looked me over, poking and joking. They took special notice of my Red Cross armband. The one who took the dog tags escorted me at gunpoint to a rather large shelter made with bamboo poles and having a roof of green leaves. He handed the tags to a man and a woman in black silk pajamas. They looked me over. The woman said, "Name?"

"Baker." She read the dog tags to see if it matched.

"Where your gun? You not soldier?"

"I'm a medic." I indicated my arm band.

The man with her said something in Vietnamese. She replied then asked, "You doctor?"

"Nurse."

"Man nurse?"

"Yes."

She spoke again to the man in charge of the camp. He said something back, indicating she should translate.

"Why you here?" she asked.

"We were sent to set up a medical station when the helicopter was shot down."

She translated for the commander. He scanned my face then spoke to her. She looked at my dog tags again.

"What this mean?" She pointed to the bottom line with the abbreviations, CO, followed by No Pref.

"It means I am a Conscientious Objector… I don't fight in war. And I don't have a religion." She translated. He spoke a couple of sentences.

She walked around me and untied my hands saying, "You work."

I wasn't sure what that meant. "I work?"

"Yes, you work here," she answered.

Then one of my captors brought my handbag and put it on the bamboo table between us. The woman dumped out the contents, razors, a toothbrush and other personal items. There was my journal and pencils, my billfold with both US money and Vietnamese script; also pictures of mom, dad, and Karen. They looked it all over. The woman held up Karen's photo, read the words on the back, and asked, "You marry?"

"No."

She scanned my Texas driver's license, showed it to the commander, pointed to it and said something. They studied the picture of mom and dad. She read and translated the words written on the back. Then the commander gave her instructions of some kind. She took the rifle off her shoulder, pointed it at me and then in the direction of a small thatched shelter. She spun me around and said, "You work there." As we were walking toward it she yelled out orders. Men began gathering all the boxes and bags of medical supplies and taking them to the shelter. It took a minute to realize this was to be my new aid station.

While we stood there watching the men bring the supplies she said, "You leave, we kill you. OK?"

"OK," I answered. Escape had already crossed my mind. But what direction would I go? How would I get through the jungle without a compass or a map? What were the chances of

143

reaching anywhere safe? What were the odds of getting caught? I couldn't think of any alternative except to cooperate and hope for rescue. But how would they find me? Could my downed chopper be seen from the air after falling into the jungle canopy? Would they even know where to search for it?

My nerves were settling somewhat but the reality of being hurt and captured was sinking in. Though remaining outwardly calm I was frantically trying to recall the POW training we received in boot camp. It seemed obvious I wasn't going to be killed or tortured unless I tried to escape or refused to work. My shoulder ached but my arm still functioned. I turned to the woman and said, "You speak English—American."

"Yes, I work embassy in Saigon, clean floor, bathroom, two year."

"My name is Ernie, Ernie Baker."

"I Khanh Ly. You call me Ly." She pointed to the boxes and said, "You work." I took that to mean begin setting up the aid station. To my surprise she turned and walked away. I started to spread out supplies on a crudely built shelf along one side of the shelter. After a minute Ly returned with a plastic jug of water.

"Food later," she said and walked away.

It was approaching midday. I organized the supplies best I could. More shelves were needed since medical goods should be off the damp ground. I found the water purification tablets and put two in the jug.

While pondering life as a captive, where I might sleep, and more importantly, how to stay alive, two men carrying another man approached. He had a badly infected left foot, from a cut. I broke down some cardboard boxes that had contained supplies and had the man lie down. The wound had to be drained, the cut stitched, and the foot wrapped. He didn't flinch during the whole process. I gave him an injection of penicillin. Before I finished the two who brought the injured man returned with a low bamboo bed. He reclined on it only a few minutes then stood and attempted to walk away. I stopped him and indicated he should wait while I assembled a set of crutches that were included in the supplies.

It never occurred that I might someday be treating enemy soldiers in a makeshift hospital in the jungle as a prisoner of war. I was grateful not to be in a POW camp, where starvation and mistreatment were the norm. At the same time, I wondered if giving "aid and comfort" to the enemy would be treasonous. It was then I remembered that bad dream, a nightmare really, about being court-martialed for treason.

Then I reflected on the nurse's oath, the Nightingale Pledge, the last line of which I very well remembered, "May my life be devoted to service and to the high ideals of the nursing profession." We were required to pledge loyalty to flag and country during induction into the army. The alternative would be disgrace, at the least, and jail at most. I decided the nurse's pledge superseded the army oath… that healing, no matter who the injured is, had always been, and would continue to be, my life's work.

Chapter 25

CAMP LIFE

The remainder of the daylight was spent organizing the supplies and hanging a mosquito net over the bamboo bed. I made a crude sort of pillow and mattress from layers of cardboard. I also treated several more minor injuries that first day. All were infected cuts. Jungle bacteria are ubiquitous and quick acting. And these poor creatures were not in the best of health. The strain of war on their bodies was obvious. No doubt they were expected to work long and hard, with improper nourishment and little rest. On top of that, many looked to be battle-weary.

When the sun was about to set Ly brought a large bowl of rice and a set of chopsticks. The rice had tiny bits of some kind of meat and small green sprouts. She said nothing but, "Eat," and started to walk away.

"When did you work at the embassy?"

She thought about it then replied, "Begin 1964, stop 1966."

"You've been out here two years?"

"Yes, two year."

She seemed not to harbor hatred or anger. She looked to be 35 to 40. "Do you have a family, children?"

"All dead. That why I Viet Cong. You no marry. No have children. Why you come here?"

"I was drafted."

"What mean drafter?"

"Drafted... I didn't ask to come to Viet Nam."

"Army tell you come here?"

146

"Yes." It was obvious communication would have to be in the simplest of words. I was very happy that she was at least able and willing to talk.

"You eat, rest."

I offered her a box of mosquito nets. She looked me in the eye, took them, and then marched off. Despite our cultural and ethnic differences I felt a friendship could develop.

To avoid detection, after the sun set no candle, lantern, or flashlights were permitted. There was a cloth poncho in the supplies; I took it and crawled under the net onto the bed and tried to sleep. As much as sleep was needed it didn't come. My body was still dealing with adrenalin from the shock of the day's events, plus my shoulder injury. I took some aspirin.

There were lots of animal noises during the night, birds and monkeys. After a while it became kind of musical. I focused on that rather than thinking about what-ifs all night. Once during the night, a shadow passed near. I assumed it was the changing of the perimeter guard. Just before morning broke I spent time praying for courage, wisdom, and perseverance. And thanking God for continuing life, something the pilot and co-pilot no longer had.

Just after sun-up the smell of boiling rice filled the air. Looking around I could see a long string of men with full battle gear entering the camp. They appeared to be very tired, like they'd marched all night. There were at least a hundred. When all had entered the camp their leader gave an order. They lined up at what I had decided must be the camp kitchen, where several large pots of rice were cooking over smokeless wood fires. Every man had a bowl and a cup in hand. I watched as the cooks gave each one a dollop, after which they dropped their gear and sat on the ground to eat. Almost nothing was said. Ly carried a large aluminum container around pouring tea.

When everyone was fed the whole group slept, leaning on their packs or lying on the ground. What a hardy bunch. Unlike their American counterparts, they certainly couldn't expect burgers and ice cream at day's end.

Over the next week it became clear this camp was a kind of rest stop for North Vietnamese Army regulars coming down the Ho Chi Minh trail to South Vietnam. It was manned and maintained by the Viet Cong. The better part of each day was spent treating their injuries and maladies. Many had the symptoms of malaria. I had nothing with which to treat it.

The NVA troops only stayed long enough for food and rest, usually eight to twelve hours. Batches showed up about every thirty-six hours. When there was no one to treat I was expected to help at the kitchen, mostly fetching water in one-gallon plastic containers from a spring on the camp's edge. Ly also carried water when not otherwise occupied. She was the only one I had spoken to since arriving, because only she spoke English. It felt strange and unnatural to be isolated by the language barrier. I thought about asking her to teach me Vietnamese, but our contact was too infrequent.

On the eighth day of captivity there were no NVA in the camp. Having nothing else to do we hauled water to the kitchen; two gallons per trip. On one of our trips that hot, muggy afternoon we stopped and sat for a moment on a big rock by the spring. She rested with arms crossed over her knees, her head on her forearms.

"Life for Viet Cong is hard," I said.

"Yes. Hard. Short," she answered without looking up.

"Are you Buddhist?"

She looked at me and said, "No. I believe Tao."

"Does the Tao teach that we live after we die?"

"I believe, yes. What you believe?"

"I believe we live."

She smiled for the first time since we met. I think we both

felt a certain spiritual kinship after that. I reckoned we shared the feeling that the hardships and uncertainties of this life are more bearable if there is life after dying. I wasn't sure how she came to believe that. Maybe her angels had shown her a vision of the next life, as mine had. I wished we could talk about this more, but the constant pressure to work, along with the lack of common language didn't permit it.

For two more weeks, the routine stayed the same. Men would come down from the north, eat, sleep, and move on. When a group arrived, there was a constant stream of injured and wounded lined up at my little aid station. Most I could help, some not. A few died and were buried outside the camp. The medical supplies were beginning to run low. I couldn't help thinking about my usefulness when they were all used up. Would more supplies come? If they didn't, would I become a kitchen slave? Or would I be sent elsewhere? When I asked Ly these questions, all she would say is, "I not know. You not worry."

I had to fight not to worry. Writing in my journal helped some. It was easy to fall into anxiety with so much uncertainty and near total absence of communication. The insights and ideas that Joyah and Rayah presented the night before I was captured kept circulating in my mind. Especially their words about the need for trying circumstances, affliction, and the inevitability of conflict. My thinking and mood continually oscillated between polar opposites; concern about the future, and faith that all things will work out for the good.

Chapter 26

RESCUE

On the twenty-second day at the camp, with no one to treat, I hauled water. Ly was nowhere to be seen. In fact, I didn't see any guards around the camp's perimeter that day. I assumed they were hunting meat, gathering firewood, or gone for rice. There didn't seem to be enough soldiers to do all that needed doing at the camp.

As I dipped a jug in the pool I heard a voice, just above a whisper, saying, "Don't look at me, pretend you hear nothing."

The first thought was that I might be imagining it. Then I heard, "Take that water back and return with more empties." My mind raced with speculation about what was happening. The man's accent was pure American. Was this a rescue? My heart leapt at the possibility. I finished filling the jugs and walked toward the kitchen trying to act like nothing had happened. No one paid me any attention. I put the water down, picked up two empty containers and walked back to the spring.

While dipping one of the jugs, without looking to see who was there, I whispered, "Who are you? What are you going to do?"

"I'm recon and rescue. I'm taking you back. Set the water down and move toward my voice. Act like you're going to take a piss."

I glanced toward the camp and didn't see anyone watching. I followed his instructions, stepping into an opening in the ground brush.

"Squat down," he ordered in low voice. "Now crawl toward me."

I crouched on my hands and knees and looked his way. He was dressed in camouflaged fatigues. His face was painted with camouflaging. He carried a small backpack, and an M-16 rifle. I could see the antenna of a radio sticking out of his pack. "Follow me. Stay low and be quiet."

He led the way, moving like an animal that lived in the jungle. He kept looking back to see if we were being followed. It was slow going; we went a long way, never saying a word. An hour passed, I estimated. Finally, we came to a clearing where a gigantic tree had fallen. He stopped near the clearing's edge. We were well hidden in the fringe brush.

"Were you the only GI there?" he asked quietly.

"Yes. My chopper pilots were killed when we crashed, three weeks ago."

"I found them. That's how I found you. I followed the trail to your camp. I've been watching you for two days."

"Who are you? Who sent you?"

"Peterson. I was sent when your bird didn't show at LZ Amy."

"Are you alone?" I asked.

"Yes. But we're getting out of here." He took out his radio and quietly spoke into the mic. "Golf bravo seven here, we're ready." He looked at his map and called out the coordinates in code. The reply came back, "Roger, on the way, golf bravo seven."

"You'll be back at Chu Lai in half an hour." That sounded like a message from heaven.

"Thanks, Peterson. You must be Green Beret or CIA?"

"Army Special Forces. And you're a CO, aren't you?"

"I am. Sorry you rescued mo?"

"Takes all kinds," he said without emotion. Soon we heard a chopper in the distance. The pilot requested a smoke grenade. Peterson took one from his pack, pulled the pin, and threw it near the center of the clearing.

It was almost unbelievable that I was being rescued. As we waited, a terrible doubt went through my mind, "What if this chopper gets shot down too?"

We moved to the center of the clearing. When the helicopter came we leapt aboard without it having to land. Then we were up and away. It felt like a great weight of uncertainty and foreboding was lifted from my shoulders. This was the first time I deeply appreciated helicopters.

While we flew, Peterson made a call over his radio. He relayed map coordinates, and then said, "Let 'er rip!"

It suddenly occurred that he was calling for a strike on Ly and the basecamp. I wanted to protest but immediately realized it would fall on deaf ears. It was, after all, an enemy basecamp. There was nothing I could do but look back and send Ly a prayer.

After a ten-minute flight, we landed at the hospital pad, right where I departed three weeks before.

Lawrence and James were there. They shook my hand and patted my back. How good it was to see them. It felt like we had been separated for much longer than three weeks.

"You don't know how to stay out of trouble, do you?" Lawrence joked.

"We weren't sure you'd be back, Ern. Don't do that again," James said.

"I have this man to thank," pointing to Peterson. They reached out and shook his hand. He acted like this is something he does every day.

"I better report in," Peterson said. He headed toward the hospital talking over his radio.

Lawrence looked at me with a smile and said, "Let's get a beer, and you can fill us in on why you went AWOL, Sergeant Baker."

James added, "We heard just a while ago that you were a POW. Where were you?"

"That beer sounds good, I'll tell you all about it" I said. "Can I get a shower and clean fatigues first?"

James said, "We got you a set of clean clothes. You can wash up in the hospital." After a quick shower and change we loaded into a jeep and headed for the USO. On the way, I told them how good Chu Lai looked. They laughed.

Lawrence replied, "All a matter of perspective, isn't it? Still looks like the same old army basecamp to these eyes. Get any ice cream or beer while you were visiting the enemy?"

"No, plenty of rice though."

Entering the USO, James said, "You're looking skinny. How about a burger and some fries? My treat."

"Make it two of each," I said.

Lawrence offered to buy the second one. I devoured them. I hadn't noticed how salty they were before. James was right, I probably lost ten pounds. After eating I sipped on the beer and chased it with ice water, then ordered chocolate ice cream. Food never tasted better.

After I told the whole story, James said he needed to go back to work. Lawrence dropped him off at the hospital then drove me to the first platoon's tent so I could report to Lieutenant Smithson. But the company was on field maneuvers, and wouldn't return for three days. Lawrence and I went to the first sergeant's clerk. He sent me in to see the first sergeant while Lawrence waited.

"Welcome back, Baker. You don't look like you're worse for the wear. Might have lost a few pounds. We got the report just yesterday that you were still alive and could return today. Smithson will be back soon. Between now and then write a detailed report. You don't need to return to duty until you're rested up. You doing OK?"

"Yes, First Sergeant. A few days rest would be good. Do you know if my parents were told I was missing?"

"Here's the letter, I was about to mail it." He wadded it up and threw it in a trashcan. "If that's all, you're dismissed."

For the next three days, I wrote and wrote. Not only a minute-by-minute report for the army, but also a long letter to mom and dad detailing my misadventure. I tried to express how much they were appreciated and how much I thought of them during the ordeal. And I told them about Karen's wedding plans. After that I filled in the journal with missing details and made a copy to send home with the letter to mom and dad.

Each of the next three nights I went into a deep sleep. No nightmares came; I was glad about that. I did dream of Ly early on the morning of the third day. We were dancing and having dinner on Mansion World One, laughing and thoroughly enjoying each other's company.

Chapter 27

SECOND ARREST

On the evening of the third day after being rescued, I handed my report over to the company clerk. On the morning of the fourth day, Company A along with Lieutenant Smithson returned to Chu Lai. I was at the hospital ready to resume duty.

Before I got to Maggie's desk to report, my fellow CO's welcomed me back, wanting to hear about being captured and rescued. They informed me that twenty-one more had become objectors during my absence. As we chatted, Maggie entered the tent and beckoned. She said, "Just got a call from Lieutenant Smithson. He wants to see you. He didn't sound happy."

"He didn't say what about?"

"No, but I think you better not return to duty just now. Go see what's on his mind first."

I thumbed a ride and found Smithson in first platoon's tent, alone, sitting at his desk. I walked up and saluted. He returned the salute and said, "At ease, Baker. Glad you made it back."

"Thank you, sir."

He had my report in his hand. He held it up and asked, "Anything to add to this?"

"No, sir. Should I?"

"You realize this is a frank admission that you aided and abetted the enemy, don't you?"

"Those are the facts as I recall them, sir."

"Sergeant, this is no small matter. If you don't amend this report, you leave me no option but to recommend that you go before a general court-martial. The maximum penalty that can be imposed by a general court-martial is death. Do you understand?"

"I don't want to change the report, sir. That's what happened."

"This is very serious, Baker. Giving aid and comfort to our enemies is considered treasonous."

I didn't know what to say. He stared at me. I assumed he was hoping I would decide to submit another report, one less inflammatory, omitting the parts about rendering aid to VC and NVA soldiers, and using US Army medical supplies to do it.

"If you let this stand, as written, the army will have no choice but to try you on the charge of aiding the enemy. You do understand the full implications of that, sergeant?"

"I think so, sir. But will the army not see that I was obliged to honor my pledge as a nurse, to treat sick and injured people, no matter who they are?"

"Did you not also pledge loyalty to your country when you entered the army?"

"Yes, sir. But I took the nurse's pledge before being drafted."

He looked exasperated, "All right Baker. Return to duty at the hospital. Your report will be handed over to HQ. Most likely this will have to go before a general court-martial... unless you want to change it." He tried to give me the report. I didn't take it.

"This will require a few days to arrange. Until then consider yourself under base arrest. Don't leave the compound. Dismissed."

It was hard to believe the army would kill or imprison me for acting as a nurse. It had crossed my mind there would be consequences. I guessed, at the worst, the army might kick me out with a dishonorable discharge. But the reality of other outcomes began to set in.

I went back to the hospital and resumed work. Two days later Maggie walked up and handed over a manila folder containing several pages. The first page was an order to appear before a pre-trial panel the next morning at 1000 hours, to determine whether a general court-martial would be convened. The charge was "Aiding and abetting the enemy with medical services and supplies." The other pages outlined the general court-martial procedure, attorney and judging options, and the range of penalties if convicted. The last page had the name of the attorney who would defend me. I called him and asked to meet.

His office was in the only air-conditioned building on the base. One of its wings had a sign over the entrance marked simply: United States Military Justice, Chu Lai. I walked down that hall looking at names on each door. I found my attorney's and knocked.

"Come in." I entered and we exchanged salutes. "At ease, Sergeant."

"Captain Gerald Le Moy." We shook hands. "Have a seat. Where you from, Baker?"

"Austin, sir."

"Where'd you take nurse's training?"

"Got my degree and license to practice at University of Texas. Then trained at Fort Sam Houston after being drafted."

"Ah, we're both UT alums. Received my law degree from there. But I grew up in San Antonio. You married? Have kids?"

"No, sir."

"Drafted and sent to Nam, were ya? My hitch will be up in two years. Will be good to get back to Texas."

"Yes, sir."

"You can drop the military protocol in here. Call me Jerry. I'll call you Ernie, OK? Let's get down to the business at hand. It's pretty serious business, you do know that?"

"I do."

"I see you have Conscientious Objector status. You're a male nurse who was drafted, trained, sent to Nam, captured, and then rescued. You've been here about seven months. During your three weeks capture, you used army medical supplies and your nursing skill to treat Viet Cong and NVA soldiers. Right so far?"

"Yes."

"The army takes this sort of thing very seriously; that's why it's probably going to a general court-martial. In cases of general court-martial, UCMJ requires that there be a pre-trial. That will happen tomorrow morning. I'll be there to represent you. If it's determined an offence against the military code of justice has been committed, a date will be set for a general. You will be formally charged and evidence will be presented to a panel of judges, or a single judge if you so choose. You understand what you're charged with, right?"

"Giving aid and comfort to the enemy."

"It's one of the most serious of all charges. You could be executed or imprisoned. Have you decided on a plea?"

"I don't dispute the charge."

"You freely admit guilt?"

"I freely admit remaining faithful to my pledge as a nurse, and the code of ethics of the nursing profession."

"I'm not sure the court will accept that, Ernie. What pledge, what code, are we talking about?"

"The Nightingale Pledge that was administered when I graduated as a nurse. The nurse's code of ethics prescribes human dignity, integrity, altruism, autonomy, and social justice."

"I'll get a copy of those from stateside. But I'm not sure the court will recognize them as valid. You also took an oath of loyalty when you were drafted. That may supersede your nursing pledge. Also, I should inform you that you are entitled to a civilian attorney since this will most likely go to a general court-martial.

If you opt for a civilian, the venue would be moved to the Pentagon."

I replied, "Let's see how the pre-trial goes... What are the chances this will advance to a general court-martial?"

"I'd say one hundred percent. You don't deny giving aid and comfort. There's no evidence against your admission. Your defense is that your nurse's oath came before and trumps your army oath, right?"

"Right."

"Tonight, I'll dig around for a precedent of your plea. And I'll go over the text of your pledge and the nurse's code of ethics. Meet me in the courtroom, at the end of this hallway, tomorrow at 1000 hours."

"Will I be allowed to speak?"

"You can, but I would advise against it unless the judges ask you to. Save that for the general court-martial." We shook hands. I thanked him and left. He seemed like a good-hearted man, certainly a sober-minded and down-the-line military man.

That evening I updated the journal and thought much about whether I was doing the right thing. I didn't want to change my plea to something that might get me off the hook or bring a lighter punishment. Neither did I relish the prospect of execution or prison. I never wanted to be a martyr, a role model, a paragon of virtue, or a traitor. I only wanted to help people be well, regardless of their role in society.

Sleep didn't come until almost sunup. During the night I prayed for wisdom, strength, and courage. I thought much about the time as a captive, and what the Guardians had said regarding the necessity and value of our earthly trials. I wanted to see them that night, but they didn't appear.

Chapter 28

PRE-TRIAL

Jerry was already at court when I arrived. We sat at a table on one side of the elongated room. The army's lawyer sat on the other side. We both faced a panel of three judges—two majors and a lieutenant colonel. The colonel hit the gavel and said, "Are the attorneys ready?" They both stood and affirmed it.

"Sergeant Baker. Do you understand you are not on trial for the charges against you, this is only a pre-trial to determine if the charges should stand?"

"I do, sir."

"How do you plead?"

Jerry replied, "Sergeant Baker does not deny the charges, sir. He does claim mitigating circumstances."

"What are they, Captain?"

"A conflict between the nurse's code of ethics and his oath as a nurse, and the army oath of loyalty and allegiance."

"And have you found precedent for such a plea?"

"No, sir."

The three judges conferred among themselves. There were several exchanges but I couldn't hear them. Then the colonel said, "Without a precedent, and with a de facto guilty plea, we find that this case should go forward to a general court-martial. The defendant has the option of hiring a civilian attorney, in which case the venue will be moved to Washington. He also has the option of having the trial here, before a panel of four officers and two enlisted men, or before a single judge appointed by the Judge Advocate's office of this basecamp. Captain Le Moy, you and your client have twenty-four hours to decide. Submit your decision to the court clerk by 1100 hours tomorrow. The defendant will not leave the basecamp. We are adjourned." He hit the gavel again.

Jerry and I went to his office. He asked, "Do you want a civilian attorney and have the trial in Washington? Or do you want to keep me as your attorney and have it here?"

"If I request a civilian attorney and the venue is moved to Washington, will I get a better hearing?"

"Depends. I couldn't really say. A lot rests on who you choose."

"Do you want to defend me? Does this case bother you? Do you think what I did was treasonous? What do you think of my plea on humanitarian grounds, and on account of my oath as a healer?"

"I thought about your situation last night. I read the nurse's pledge and code of ethics, and came to the conclusion that I would have done the same thing in your place."

"Then I'd like to keep you as my representative." I felt a fraternal bond with him. He seemed like someone I could trust to do his best. "Which of the judging panel options do you recommend?"

"I think you might fare better if we go with four officers and two enlisted men. You have two buddies who would be willing to sit on the panel?"

"I do." Lawrence and James came to mind.

"All right. I'll submit your decision to the clerk tomorrow. We'll wait for a date. It should happen soon, I think the army wants this case expedited. As soon as I hear, I'll send word."

I went back to work at the hospital. That night Rayah and Joyah appeared during the wee hours. After exchanging joyful greetings Rayah teased me saying, "Well, Ernie, you may be going to the mansion worlds very soon!"

I said, "This is not a big deal to you, is it?" We laughed. "Are you suggesting that I would be smarter to ask for death instead of prison?"

Joyah replied, "If prison is the result of your trial, you will endure."

"And if the court decides I should cease living?"

Rayah answered, "We don't think that will be the verdict. We believe you made the right choice of judges."

"You know something I don't?"

"Let's leave it at that," Joyah said with a warm smile. I drew hope from her reply. Then she added, "But if you were sentenced to die, you would soon find yourself on the mansion worlds, and in a new body, one not of flesh and bone, but of a more enduring substance. Tonight, we felt it would be appropriate to enlighten you and cheer you with more insights into your next life."

Rayah said, "You'll recall we informed you of the progressive nature of the mansion training regime… that there are seven mansion worlds, each one a step higher on the spiritual ladder. And on each one you will learn from those just ahead and teach those just behind, assisted by a permanent staff of teachers. Not all beings there will be ascending, like you. Some are created specifically to serve ascenders. They remain as you move forward in your soul's evolution."

Joyah continued, "On the first mansion world you will take up life precisely where you left off on Earth. There are no short cuts to character growth and spiritual attainment. The only differences you will notice are the acquirement of a new body, and your presence on a dissimilar world, one constructed solely for the purpose of schooling ascending angels such as yourself. You will never forget, in all your ascendant life, awakening in Resurrection Hall, in a fresh body, and on another world."

Rayah went on, "When you arrive, you will be granted ten days of liberty. During that time, you will be permitted to consult the registry of persons, the record of all who are present or have passed through the mansion worlds. There you may find the location and status of relatives and friends who preceded you in death. You may travel, explore, and visit anywhere or anyone on

Mansion One during your ten-day liberty. All the magnificent temples of that sphere will be open to you for communal worship, a place to meet others on equal footing in spiritual firmament. And you will encounter many types of beings in temples and elsewhere, including Mansion World Companions. These unique beings are charming associates and competent guides. They will lead you on excursions and help orient you to life as an ascendant pilgrim. They are members of the permanent staff of which I spoke."

Joyah continued, "On the second mansion world you will join other ascenders to form a class. Class formation is standard practice for ascension candidates. Here all associations are friendly and fraternal. As you ascend, world-by-world, your body will undergo adjustments, the first of which occurs on Mansion Two. Your personality will remain the same throughout, but your form will change, becoming more spiritual and less physical. Memory, but not worthless memories, will remain intact. Everything of spiritual value—your relationships, and your indwelling fragment of God, your personality—these are your permanent possessions. The focus of training on Mansion Two is primarily intellectual; it is a preparation of your mind for the spiritual challenges that lie ahead."

Then Rayah talked about Mansions Three and Four, "On the third sphere you will encounter teachers of cosmic meanings and universe interrelations. There is a school of what you might refer to as 'super-philosophy,' a kind of logic that combines wisdom, experience, and cosmic revelation. On the fourth mansion world, you will have the opportunity to apply much of what you have learned about social situations on the lower spheres. As Joyah said, ascending survivors are grouped into classes that rise together, ever working for greater harmonization of relationships. It is here that the motive to love overtakes the desire for self-aggrandizement, where mutual appreciation and service are born of a greater understanding of God's primary motivation, the divine affection that pervades and propels the Universe of Universes."

Joyah gave these insights about Mansions Five and Six: "After the physical, intellectual, and social training of the first four mansions you will begin to learn the languages of the higher realms. You will acquire new word meanings up there just as you do on Earth. Your ever-progressing mind will assimilate new knowledge... at the same time you will be introduced to numerous other types of beings, from angels to administrators. Mansion Five is the world where you experience the birth of true cosmic consciousness, where you become universe-minded. Here you begin to recognize the immensity of the cosmos and your unique place in it. On Mansion Six you will begin to visualize some of the higher beings of the universe, and you will gain insights into life beyond and above the mansions. Here you receive your first lessons about the whole creation. And often, it is here that the immortal soul and the divine indweller find *union*, harmonious attunement of ascending mortal with descending God."

Rayah finished the night's instruction saying, "And finally, on the seventh mansion world, you will receive wise instruction from many teachers. You begin on the first mansion as a mostly physical being. On the seventh, you are, for the most part, spiritual in nature, character, and constitution. And here you will be given insight into the next phase of your cosmic career. The mansion world regime is often referred to as being part of the *System*. Your next and higher adventure is in the *Constellation*. Life at the Constellation level takes up right where you left off at the System."

Joyah added in parting, "Never doubt that we will be near as you face your accusers during the coming days. Before your trial seek advice in prayer and comfort in worship. Always remember that worship is a source of divine creativity—and that prayer is a limitless fount of cosmic insight. As events unfold listen for the inner leading, the 'small, still, voice' that always knows what to say, always knows how to respond to such questions as will soon confront you."

Chapter 29

COURT-MARTIAL

It was six days after the pre-trial that the summons was issued. Lawrence and James agreed to be on the judging panel of my court-martial. The court-martial was to take place the next day in the same room as the pre-trial. Jerry briefed me on what to expect the day before, saying my rescuer, Peterson, would testify for the prosecution. We decided that it would be best if I also testified. He advised getting a haircut, a close shave, going to the camp quartermaster for a Class A uniform, and wearing the insignias for my two Purple Hearts, and the Bronze Star.

Jerry and I were seated when the court session opened. We came to attention when the judges entered. They were right on time and took a seat behind long, narrow, folding tables at the front of the room. There were four officers: one bird colonel, one major, and two captains. Lawrence and James sat at the end of table.

"At ease." We sat, then the colonel whispered something to the major, then hit the table with the gavel and said, "Let the record show this is a general court-martial. The United States Army versus Sergeant Ernie Ross Baker on the charge of rendering aid and comfort to the enemy during combat operations in Vietnam while serving in the American Division, 5th Brigade, 2nd Battalion, Company A, as a medic. Captain Gerald Le Moy was appointed as the defendant's attorney, Captain Franklin Georges is serving as prosecutor. I, Colonel John Ashcraft, am serving as lead judge." As he spoke a corporal typed his words on a court-recorder.

The colonel then said, "Captain Georges, state the army's case."

"Yes, Colonel. I would submit for the court's review a copy of Sergeant Baker's report of his three weeks as a captive of the enemy. In this report, he states that he rendered aid and comfort

165

to both Viet Cong and North Vietnamese Army soldiers in the form of medical treatment and services. He further states he used US Army medical supplies to render this aid. At no time did he refuse to give such aid, and never did he attempt to escape. The army charges this constitutes a violation of the Uniform Code of Military Justice regarding the conduct of prisoners of war."

"Captain Le Moy, does the defendant deny the charge?"

"No, Colonel. But the defense would stipulate that war has not been declared. And further that Sergeant Baker became a licensed nurse before he entered the army as a draftee. On completion of his course of training as a nurse he made a pledge, known as the Nightingale Pledge. He also swore an oath to the Nurse's Code of Ethics. The defense would submit a copy of the Nightingale Pledge for the court's review."

"The court will allow it," said the colonel. "Read the text relevant to this case for the court recorder, Captain Le Moy." Jerry handed a copy to each of the judges and the prosecutor.

"Yes, Colonel. The Nightingale Pledge states as follows:

'Before God and those assembled here, I solemnly pledge; To adhere to the code of ethics of the nursing profession; To co-operate faithfully with the other members of the nursing team and to carry out faithfully and to the best of my ability the instructions of the physician or the nurse who may be assigned to supervise my work; I will not do anything evil or malicious and I will not knowingly give any harmful drug or assist in malpractice. I will not reveal any confidential information that may come to my knowledge in the course of my work. And I pledge myself to do all in my power to raise the standards and prestige of the practical nursing; May my life be devoted to service and to the high ideals of the nursing profession.'

"Colonel, the Nurse's Code of Ethics is forty pages. The defense would submit this copy for the court's review." Jerry laid it before the colonel, saying, "If it pleases the court, I would read certain germane parts of Provision 1 as primary examples of the code's content?"

"Proceed, Captain," answered Ashcraft.

"Provision 1.1 is titled, 'Respect for Human Dignity.' It reads:

'A fundamental principle that underlies all nursing practice is the inherent worth, dignity and human rights of every individual. Nurses take into account the values and needs of all persons in all professional relationships.'

"Provision 1.2 has the title, 'Relationships to Patients'. It states:

'The need for health care is universal, transcending all individual differences. The nurse establishes relationships and delivers nursing services with respect for human needs and values, and without prejudice. An individual's lifestyle, value system and religious beliefs should be considered in planning health care with and for each patient. Such consideration does not suggest that the nurse necessarily agrees with or condones certain individual choices, but that the nurse respects the patient as a person.'" Jerry then took his seat.

"Does the prosecution have witnesses to call?" asked Ashcraft.

Georges replied, "Colonel, the prosecution calls Staff Sergeant Matthew Peterson." Ashcraft ordered Peterson to take the witness chair and administered the oath. Georges requested that he state his name and rank for the record, and then asked, "Sergeant Peterson, it was you who located and rescued Sergeant Baker, correct?"

"Yes, sir."

"And did you observe Sergeant Baker's activities before you effected the rescue?"

"Yes, sir, for two days I watched from outside the camp where he was held, through binoculars."

"And what did you observe?" Georges asked.

"I watched Baker giving medical treatment to several NVA's. When he wasn't treating enemy soldiers, he was assisting the camp cook, hauling water."

"And during this two days of observation, did you note any coercion, any threats against him or others if he didn't render this assistance?"

"No, sir. None."

"Thank you, Sergeant Peterson."

Ashcraft then asked, "Does the defense wish to question this witness?"

Jerry stood and asked, "Sergeant Peterson, do you have any reason to believe that Sergeant Baker willingly volunteered to treat the wounded who were brought to him, or that he wanted to haul water?"

Peterson hesitated a moment, then answered, "No, sir."

Jerry went on, "And when you rescued him, did he resist or otherwise indicate he wished to stay and continue performing nursing services for the enemy?"

"No, sir."

"Thank you, Sergeant. That's all, Colonel."

Ashcraft asked Georges, "Do you have other witnesses or testimony, Captain?"

"No, Colonel."

"Captain Le Moy, does the defense have witnesses or testimony it wishes to present?"

"Yes, Colonel. The defense would call the defendant."

"Take the chair, Sergeant Baker," Ashcraft ordered. I swore the truth oath.

Jerry's first question was, "What were the circumstances of your capture, Sergeant Baker?"

"An order was issued to set up an aid station at Landing Zone Amy. I was on the way with medical supplies when the helicopter was shot down in the foothills of the jungle west of Chu Lai. The pilot and co-pilot were killed. The helicopter lodged sideways in the trees. I fell to the ground. Boxes of medical supplies were under me and kept me from being injured in the fall. Very soon I heard voices speaking Vietnamese; several men were approaching. I hid but was discovered. They took me to a jungle camp about a kilometer away. I stayed there for three weeks, until Sergeant Peterson rescued me."

"What did you do while you were captive?"

"Just as Peterson said, I treated injuries and wounds. And when there was no one to treat, I carried water."

"Was it your desire to perform these services?"

"No, sir. I was told what to do by the camp commander."

"And if you didn't comply?"

"There was little doubt the consequences would be prison or death."

"Did you never consider escaping?"

"I did consider it. But without a compass, a map, or knowledge of where I was, chances of a successful escape were not promising. And in the event of a recapture, chances of survival would not be good. I was told I'd be killed for trying to escape."

"Were you not aware that your actions constituted aid to the enemy?"

"That crossed my mind. I realized there was a conflict. And I knew that if I refused to do as told, the consequences would be imprisonment at best, torture and death at worst. I also thought about the conflict between my oath as a nurse and my oath to country. I thought if I survived, I could report the deaths of the pilots, and that I could go back to serving my country at the hospital. I asked myself, would the army be better off with me dead or alive?"

"Did you honestly think your nurse pledge superseded your army oath?"

"I did, and still I do."

Jerry then asked, "You're a Conscientious Objector, are you not?"

"Yes, sir."

"Did that have any bearing on your decision to perform nursing services while in captivity?"

"Well, it's my underlying motive to help rather than harm. That's why I became a nurse. I sought CO status because I don't believe killing and maiming is the right way to solve international, or personal, differences."

"Before you volunteered to set up the medical station at LZ Amy, what services did you perform for the army?"

"I worked at the base hospital, as manager of a group of CO's whose job is to help with the care of the wounded and injured."

"And how many of your fellow soldiers do you think you treated during your time at the base hospital?"

"Hundreds, I'd guess."

"How many NVA did you treat, would you say?"

"Scores, maybe more. I would guess on average a half-dozen a day."

"Before you were captured, and before you worked at the hospital, what did you do?"

"Right after arriving in country, I went with my company on maneuvers in the field, as a medic."

"And you were awarded two Purple Hearts as a result of injuries sustained while serving as a medic?"

"Yes, sir."

Jerry turned to the panel and said, "The court is advised that Sergeant Baker also received a Bronze Star for service above and beyond the call, which was rendered during a beach incursion here at Chu Lai. One man's life was saved by his actions during that attack."

"Sergeant Baker, was it your intention to harm your country by giving aid to its enemies?"

"No, sir."

"What was your intention?"

"My intention was, and always has been, to give aid to anyone who needs it. It's what I dedicated my life to."

"Thank you, Sergeant," Jerry took his seat.

Ashcraft said, "Does the prosecutor have questions for the accused?"

Georges stood and said, "Yes, Colonel. Sergeant Baker, while you were helping the enemy, did it occur to you that one or more of the men you treated might go on to wound or kill one or more of our men?"

"Sir, I knew that was a possibility. But I also thought it possible that the ones I treated might, under certain circumstances, return the favor. Who's to say one of them could, some day, be a guard at a POW camp where Americans are held, or otherwise hold the life of one of ours in his hands? As their captive, they could plainly see I was not that much different from them, just another man caught up in a brutal conflict, away from home and family."

Then he asked, "Sergeant, there are now over a hundred Conscientious Objectors at Chu Lai basecamp, and more apply every week. How many of those did you counsel, encourage, or abet?"

Jerry stood up, "Objection, Colonel. Irrelevant to this proceeding."

"I'll allow it, Captain. You may answer, Sergeant."

"Sir, the only counseling I offered was to tell those who asked what was required, and where to apply. I did no encouraging or abetting."

"Sergeant Baker, were you not also arrested for possessing an opium pipe while working as a leader of the so-called, 'Baker's Brigade,' composed of Conscientious Objectors?"

Jerry rose to his feet and said loudly, "Objection, Colonel! Not relevant to this proceeding." He leaned over and I whispered that the charges were dismissed when it was revealed that I was framed.

"Colonel, Sergeant Baker was cleared of that charge when it was discovered the pipe was planted. It is disingenuous for the prosecution to bring it into court."

The colonel looked at him questioningly, "Captain Georges?"

He changed the subject. "Sergeant Baker, would you read the oath you took on entering the army?" He handed me a piece of teletype paper.

"I, Ernie Baker, do solemnly affirm that I will support and defend the Constitution of the United States against all enemies, foreign and domestic; that I will bear true faith and allegiance to the same; and that I will obey the orders of the President of the United States and the orders of the officers appointed over me, according to regulations and the Uniform Code of Military Justice. So help me God."

"Is this your signature?"

"Yes, Sir."

"Would you please explain to the court how an oath to God and country outweighs a nurse's pledge?"

"God and country are the reasons I did what I did. When

I prayed to know what God would do in my place, I felt the answer was to care for the sick and injured, no matter who. Thinking about doing right by my country, I decided the highest good anyone can do is to be an honorable representative of both God and country...I've always thought that God would find a better way to settle international disputes than war."

He looked perplexed and stepped back to consult with his associates for a long moment.

"No further questions, Colonel. The prosecution rests."

Ashcraft looked at both attorneys and asked, "Nothing else, Captains?"

Jerry stood and said, "Sergeant Baker, your opinion of the army's role in this conflict might bear on the judges' decisions. Before they go to their deliberations, explain to the full court your justification for this apparent act of collusion with our foes."

I thought for a moment and replied, "I'm not unsympathetic to the army's point of view. It has been given an impossible mission, and expected to accomplish it mostly with unwilling men who have sensed the war is already lost, and all they want to do is endure a year and make it home whole. In such a situation, the best support I can offer my country is to refuse to fight, but agree to serve any and all of those injured in war."

"Anything to ask or add, Captain Georges?"

"No, sir."

After a moment, the colonel said, "The court will adjourn. The judges will retire to confer on a verdict. A decision will be forthcoming. The defendant is to remain under camp arrest." He struck the table with his gavel, picked up the copies of the pledge and the code and turned to walk out. Lawrence and James looked my way as they left the room with the four officers.

Jerry and I went to his office. I asked, "When will we know?"

"Soon, probably. I know those officers. They are men of few words. Why don't we wait here awhile, in case the judge reconvenes the hearing today."

We went for a cup of coffee at the front desk and returned to his office. While waiting we discussed the war, the army's role in it, and his family—a wife and three kids. Being a career officer meant a lot of time overseas, and out of touch.

Forty-five minutes passed. Then the court clerk knocked on the door, stuck his head in, and said, "Verdict's in. The colonel called everyone back to the courtroom."

We stood at attention when the judges entered and sat. The colonel said, "At ease men. It is the determination of this court, by a vote of four to two, that Sergeant Ernie Baker shall not be convicted on the charge of rendering aid and comfort to the enemy. Let the record reflect this decision. The defendant will return to duty without reduction in rank or pay, and receive an honorable discharge providing there are no other convictions or incriminating circumstances. We are adjourned." The gavel sounded a final time.

Jerry shook my hand. Two of the judges scowled at me; easy to guess they had voted against acquittal. It was a huge relief and I offered a silent prayer of thanksgiving. Breathing easier now that it was over, and vindication was the result, I invited Lawrence and James to a celebratory round of burgers and beer. While we walked to the USO they told me there was bitter disagreement between the two officers who voted against, and the two who voted for conviction. It was Lawrence and James' persuasion and vote that swung the verdict my way.

Chapter 30

VISITING MANSONIA

Working at the base hospital during the following months, all went as well as could be expected in a war zone. The casualties never ceased. In fact, their number increased. And the number of objectors continued to rise. As more and more helpers became available, Maggie had Lawrence, James, and me, training them in operating room chores, assisting with triage, and manning the medivac choppers going out in the field to remove the wounded. She assigned all duties at the base morgue to us; we were responsible for collecting details and circumstances of fallen men and passing them on to senior officers who wrote their families.

James, Lawrence, and I became close friends and working associates while serving together in Nam. It was with both considerable sadness and great joy that I said so long to them in mid-January of '69. James departed first; Lawrence and I took him to the heliport and saw him off. Two days later I did the same for Lawrence. My last two months in country felt a bit lonely without them.

We three kept in touch, and arranged periodic reunions where much laughter and reminiscing took place. At a recent reunion, I told James and Lawrence, for the first time, about my encounters with the Guardians, and that a book would be coming out soon. Neither of them seemed shocked or bothered; in fact Lawrence immediately gave a clever, "Write on!" And, once again, they gave me a mocking bow, this time to "saint, and soon-to-be author, Ernie." Old friendships are the best friendships.

James became an air traffic controller in Albany, then found Ms. Right and raised a big family, four girls and five boys. Lawrence married a tenured professor and became one himself, teaching comparative philosophy at Arizona State University;

175

they had only one child, a girl. And I received a letter from Maggie after she finally retired, saying over 1100 CO's served at the hospital before the war ended in '75. We spoke often, but never met again. She died in '99.

Every week or two after my rescue, Mailee and I exchanged letters. About two months after R&R, she wrote to say she was offered an internship at a large Bangkok hospital, and that the hospital would pay for the remainder of her schooling. She was overjoyed; so was I. And I got a good laugh in that letter. She included a painted picture of a group of red roosters crowing at the setting moon. I still have it, framed on my desk, at home.

During the night before I was to leave Vietnam, my Guardians appeared while I slept. Our greeting was especially warm and touching. Their embrace filled me with that angelic love I had come to expect and so appreciate.

Joyah said, "Congratulations, Ernie. You will long remember the moving events and strange adventures of the year just passed. Many were the trials and tests of your character and your willingness to persevere. We are pleased with your spiritual progress and personal development over this period. You have proven yourself worthy of our respect. We feel quite certain you will finish carrying out your part of our mission. When you return home, safeguard your notes and your journal entries. At the appropriate time you will publish this record of the war and your angelic contact—all that we revealed during your tour of duty. We wish to offer one last installment while you are here, one more testament to the next life. You are about to experience what you refer to as heaven. A preview, if you will."

Rayah said, "Rather than trying to describe the mansion worlds, it will be much more effective and enlightening to offer a view. We have been granted permission to provide you with a vision of the place of resurrection, and some features of the first mansion world, where mortals awaken after departing life on Earth. There you will be in a better place, and in a new bodily form. What you are about to witness is real. And you are destined to find yourself there, continuing life that began here, in the flesh. Indeed, life on Earth is but the entrance gate to this greater, more robust eternal life."

Joyah and Rayah each took one of my hands and peered intensely into my eyes. After a second or two, images began to form in my mind. At first, things were quite blurry and unfocused. Soon the vision sharpened and clarified. I could see oddly shaped buildings, but they looked bright and clean, made of super-shiny metals and what appeared to be translucent, crystal-like material. I looked up at the sky. It was a bright blue with no sun, clouds, moon, or stars. Light seemed to emanate from everywhere. I could sense something right and whole, something indefinably wonderful. Feelings of awe and joy filled me. All I wanted to do was absorb and keep that rightness, and its wholeness.

"This *is* heaven, isn't it?" I said in complete and utter astonishment.

"Only the first heaven, Ernie," Rayah said. "Behold the world on which you will someday reside, when your course on Earth has been run." My vision widened, my focus sharpened. I could see there were beings moving around. Some looked rather human, and others appeared much like my Guardians.

Ever more sights and sounds sprang to mind—I reeled a bit. Everything was so rich and pristine. Every surface, everything stationary, was gleaming, artistically arranged and embellished. There was movement and activity everywhere. Some were walking; many were being transported inside flying vehicles that might be best described as oval pods. They were large and small, like an egg on its side, and they were transparent. They glided along very fast, but without apparent propulsion.

I looked up and saw a person riding atop a great bird. "There are animals here? Flying ones that can be ridden?!"

"Many are the wonders you will encounter here, Ernie," Joyah assured me. It was beyond thrilling to witness all this.

Then that scene faded and another appeared. Rayah said, "And this is where mortals resurrect after life in the flesh. This is Resurrection Hall." Looking around I could see thousands upon thousands of individual chambers, small gleaming-white enclosures, some were occupied with beings exchanging gleeful greetings and having joyous reunions. Some were vacant. I couldn't help comparing what I was seeing with a hospital's maternity ward.

Rayah told me, "When your life on Earth is finished, one of these chambers is where your soul will be reunited with the divine entity that indwelt you as a human. The soul, the personality, and that entity are here reassembled, housed in a new form about which we spoke."

As she said that, three beings strolled by quite close. They were conversing in a language I didn't understand. Their bodies were covered with close fitting, shimmering cloth that slightly shifted in color as they moved. I was transfixed. They didn't seem to notice my stare.

"Can they see or hear us?" I asked.

"No. What you see and hear now is for your edification alone. You may not, at this time, interact on the mansion worlds—not until you actually resurrect here in this great hall. Joyah and I are able to project this vision, these sounds, to your mind. But this is an actual reality you are witnessing. What you are viewing is unfolding now on Mansion World Number One, inside the walls of Resurrection Hall."

Those high walls were capped with promenades. They surrounded the immense resurrection arena. Many beings were strolling atop these promenades. Some had stopped and were perched on the bejeweled guardrail, simply observing the vast resurrection area.

Then Joyah said, "Ernie, revelations and visions of Mansonia are not unprecedented. Many who attained higher spiritual understanding during life on Earth were also granted a vision of what awaits mortal survivors on Mansonia. Especially is this true toward the end of a well-led life in the flesh. You are an obvious exception."

Next they presented another view, outside the hall. In all directions I saw amazing plants, lovely and artistically arranged landscapes. There were also huge structures of astonishing beauty and magnificent construction; it wasn't clear what they were. Questions popped into my mind by the dozen. I had to pause to take in the wonder of it all.

Beings somewhat alike, but every one unique, were moving about almost everywhere. All were of like design. But somehow the substance wasn't the same, not meat and bone-like, perhaps more like energy. And I could actually sense a joyfulness of fellowship with diverse personalities that is mostly absent on Earth. I couldn't stop staring and marveling at the incredible, remarkable, jaw-dropping sights everywhere, both living and material.

"I didn't know heaven would or could be like this. I like it!" I felt like laughing and so I did. My Guardians laughed with me. It was a genuine joy to view these scenes. The more I saw of Mansion One, the more I noticed everything was beautifully crafted, detailed, and adorned. There was plant life everywhere, gigantic trees with branches, leaves, and flowers that were all shades of violet and blue and green. Many of the plants, great and small, were bearing fruit. These fruits, hanging and on the ground, were highly diverse in both size and color. I had never seen or imagined such shapes and hues before.

It was all so very real, yet so unreal, or at least unfamiliar. It was mesmerizing watching the human-like beings strolling— and others transporting in the airborne pods. A definite fraternity seemed to pervade this world. I thought, 'Love and peace are palpable here. Earth could be like this someday.' A certain

179

fearlessness and openness was apparent. It was all but intoxicating. I felt giddy for a short moment.

Then I began to look closely at buildings near and far. Every one gleamed and exuded a celestial radiance in beauty, form, artistry, and color. Best I could tell from that vantage point, almost every building lacked a top. Shiny walls were present, but no roofs. The walls themselves all had aesthetically pleasing and highly artistic embellishments. I decided that beauty isn't an afterthought on Mansion One; it is a theme.

"Aren't there roofs here?" I asked.

"Not needed," said Rayah. "There is no wet or windy weather on constructed worlds. The light, heat, and irrigation systems are built in, part of the design."

"Constructed?"

"The mansion spheres and all their appointments are created on purpose by beings whose work it is. They create heavenly blueprints you might say. They plan the atmosphere and all else that pertains to the needs and maintenance of mansion life," Joyah replied.

"The mansion worlds aren't made of dirt and rock, with a hot core? There's no rain? No lightening, thunder, floods? What about earthquakes? I mean, mansion-quakes."

"None of those, Ernie. This sphere, indeed all of the mansions, are built to divine specifications. They are known as 'architectural spheres' and are unlike the evolutionary planets such as Earth. They are made of materials, some known to you, and some unknown. On your world there are approximately one hundred elements. On the architectural spheres, there are two hundred. The atmosphere, light, and temperature, are all intentionally designed, built to order, constantly monitored, and efficiently controlled," Rayah answered. "Power to do all this is drawn from the ever-present energies of surrounding space, and by techniques that would astound Earth scientists."

"This *is* a different sort of world," I uttered in total amazement. "There is air here, to breathe… and to fly in."

Joyah answered, "On the mansion worlds the atmosphere is perfectly composed to support your new semi-physical form. Here bodies are sustained by a three-gas mixture. The large transport bird you saw is able to fly you through the air at a hundred miles per hour, as distance and time are measured on Earth."

The scene shifted again. I saw a charming cottage tucked under three majestic trees, all with violet leaves and draped in tiny, baby-blue blossoms. Rayah said, "This is the residence of your grandparents."

I looked my angels in their adorable faces and said, "How beautiful. This is all too good to be true."

It too had no roof. Everything inanimate shone and gleamed, exuding a kind of luster that could only be described as precious. I was taken inside. The furniture, tables and chairs, all were made of bright and beautiful metals, upholstered in shimmering fabrics, inlaid with a variety of bright jewels. A kind of reflective crystal embellished many surfaces.

A small, ornate, gold fountain flowed steadily into a crafted drain basin in one corner. To my eyes every article and item was well appointed and in the right place. I had a flash of memory of my grandparent's home on Earth. It was something like this, but quaint compared to their miniature mansion here, designed and adorned as it was.

"It's quite an improvement on homes of Earth, would you say?" Joyah remarked.

"An improvement that's stretching my ability to grasp!" I exclaimed. "Where are Nana and Grandad?"

"They are away, on excursion to another world," Rayah replied. "And yes, we know this experience—this revelation— can overawe humans. But try to relax and fill your memory with these visions. They have the power to bolster and inform you in the face of difficulties that are sure to come during the remainder of your life in the flesh."

"All right, I will remember," I assured the Guardians. "And I'm especially happy to know that we will *not* be stuck on one world."

"The higher one ascends, the greater the freedom of movement and exploration. This first mansion world may seem like heaven to you, but there are many heavens above it, and far greater in beauty and allure. As you ascend, sphere-by-sphere, you will progress in spirit, grow in character, and accumulate increasing wisdom through enhanced meanings and values. You will acquire experiences that are now unimaginable. And you should remember that the yoke of heaven is easy. About half the time you will be free to play, to travel, and to create. The other half you will perform teamwork, learn new concepts and pursue ever greater ideals, so that you might assist those coming up behind you. We haven't the least doubt that you will fit in very well here, Ernie," Rayah assured me.

Suddenly I felt a surge of pure happiness, at the sheer wonder of it all, and the fact that I would someday live here. It truly felt like I was in heaven. "It's going to take a while to get used to this. Heaven is real, and I have seen it," I declared. Amazement and joy filled my mind and surely showed on my face.

I asked about the fountain. "Is that water? We drink water here?"

Joyah answered, "It is the same as the water back on Earth. But when you arrive here, you will taste it with new senses."

"Will I eat too?"

"On the mansion worlds you will breathe, drink, and eat. The food is of a different order, but water is the same everywhere," replied Rayah.

"When you are resurrected in new form, you will find all the old senses have improved. Taste, smell, vision, and hearing, are greatly expanded. And you will have yet other sensory abilities, unknown and unimagined in your present estate."

We began to rise over Nana and Grandad's roofless cottage. Joyah pointed to a lush garden in back saying, "Your grandparents created this." It was truly living artistry. Remarkably beautiful plants were bearing a dazzling variety of produce. Then I remembered being a kid and enjoying the great meals they served when we visited their little farm with its vegetable garden and fruit trees. I tried to imagine what dishes Nana and Grandad might create from this garden, and how wonderful they might taste.

We floated into the garden. There were many rows, some very high, some growing in large clumps on the surface. I saw a great variety of unfamiliar plants and trees; all had leaves and vines of radiant colors, some familiar and some I can't describe. Most were bearing what I assumed to be plump fruits and giant vegetables. Then, suddenly, I smelled rich layers of fragrance. From the flowers, I assumed.

As I bathed in the sights and smells, I thought of those other mansions Joyah mentioned. "You said there are seven mansion worlds of ascending beauty, and more beyond that. I don't know how they can be greater than this."

"There are worlds beyond worlds, Ernie, each greater than the last. On none of them will you become old, sick, or lose your memory. Gradually you will become accustomed to the idea of life eternal, endless youth and progressing spirituality, until you finally and fully achieve perfection of being and status. Perfection is the ultimate goal of every ascending being.

"There is much more that will be revealed when you actually take up life here. And you will not be deprived of any avenue or method that helps you advance toward your worthy goals across time and eternity," Joyah declared.

Then I thought to ask what must be a common question, "I'm curious... on the mansion worlds, will we make love, I mean, have sex?" They both smiled with empathy and understanding.

"Every ascender wants to know that after acquiring and examining their new body," Rayah told me.

Joyah elaborated, "Since there is no need for procreation, mansion world pilgrims have no need for reproductive organs. Also, you will not have to eliminate food waste anymore. The cosmically energized bodies of resurrected beings are designed to utilize everything ingested; the kind of food you will consume produces no waste matter."

"How can all this be true? But I believe you! I can hardly wait to be reborn here. Will I still be a man? I noticed that some beings appear to be female and some male. Why is that... if we don't have sex?"

Rayah said, "Male and female are down-stepped universal patterns, derived from our Creator Parents. Surviving mortals retain their gender identity. But the simple pleasures of sex are replaced by a higher kind of intimacy, a kind that is largely unknown on the mortal level. Here, you can still 'make love' as you refer to it. And you will discover so much that is new and thrilling about personal relationships on the mansion worlds. You may recall hearing these words during your youth, 'In resurrection neither will they marry, but they are like the angels of heaven.'"

"I do remember that verse. But I never stopped to think what gender and intimacy might be like in the next life."

"Now, Ernie, you have an expanded view and understanding of mansion life," Rayah said.

"Yes, indeed! And I have to thank you. But, I keep thinking, what is there to do on the mansions? I haven't seen anyone sitting on a cloud playing a harp. But, from what I've seen, they move around a lot. I get the feeling there is a great deal going on here. Obviously, those gardens don't grow themselves. What are the days like? And how long is a day? Are there nights too? I have a thousand questions, maybe more. And the more you reveal the more questions I have."

"There is much to know and learn, so much to do and become. When you resurrect in new form you will first receive a brief orientation about the basics of mansonia life. And immediately thereafter you will have ten days to explore Mansion World One without restriction. The day, on all seven mansions, is three times as long as the day is on the Earth. And yes, there is a night season in which all rest and recoup their energies." As Joyah said that, the vision of Mansion One faded.

Rayah closed the session with these words. "Ernie, we are grateful you became a willing volunteer, helping carry out our assigned mission. We very much appreciate the willingness you have displayed thus far. The final phase will be to report to others what you have seen and learned during these nocturnal visits.

"Never doubt we are always near, Ernie. We are with you always. And for as long as you remain on Earth we will, periodically, be in direct contact. Just as we were during this eventful year. We are hoping you will permit us to help you refine and organize your report, before it is published aboard."

"I believe you. I want and need your help," I said with complete honesty.

We three shared a long and endearing embrace, another one I never forgot.

Chapter 31

ROTATION HOME

On the last day at the hospital, while clearing out my desk, Maggie walked up and delivered orders to "rotate," army lingo for going home. "It won't be as easy without you, Ernie. I have to thank you for an abundance of helping hands around here. A lot of bleeding men were helped by the efficient and humane care you and your objector brigade rendered."

"You're the best Major Boss in the army, Maggie. Thanks for everything; you've been a rock in a storm. When do you get to go home?"

"This is home. It's where I'm needed. It's where I can do some good in the midst of so much bad. Hey, why don't you re-up? I'll swing my considerable weight around to see that you're stationed right here in nurse's paradise."

"That is very tempting Maggie, but I'm going back to school. Maybe nurse Baker will be doctor Baker for the next war. Then I can be your boss." We laughed, then hugged tightly. "May I send you anything from stateside?"

"Yeah, send more objectors. Can't have too many. It looks like this war will go on for a while."

I'll never forget how beautiful she looked as I walked out of the Chu Lai hospital for the last time, standing there in army fatigues with smiling eyes and reddish-gray wisps of ponytail hair gently lifted and tossed by the breeze.

I went to the company clerk to leave a copy of the rotation orders. The first sergeant came out of his office to shake hands. He said, "Why don't you make the army a career, Baker? Otherwise you'll be known as a draftee all your life." We chuckled. It was the first time I recall hearing him laugh.

As I was walking out of the tent, Lieutenant Smithson was coming in. He stopped and said, "I have a friend who gets a fat

186

bonus when a draftee re-ups, Sergeant Baker. And the reenlistment bonus is up to ten-grand now. And, you know, it's getting more dangerous stateside than here." But he knew the answer was no. He shook my hand and said, "Take care, Sergeant."

"I will, Lieutenant. And don't you worry, I won't tell anyone about your missing toe." He smiled, then hugged me ever so briefly.

The last helicopter ride was to Cam Ranh Bay Airport. There I was processed out with hundreds of others and put on a commercial plane. The Boeing 707 was full, every seat taken by military personnel, all grunts like me. As we gathered speed to take off, anticipation of leaving Vietnam behind and going home was growing in our hearts, minds, and souls. When our flight left the ground, a cheer like I've never heard before or since broke out. It started in the back of the plane and moved to the front. Surely every man was thinking, hoping, and praying, "Don't let this plane be shot down." The cheering went on, louder and louder. Every man had his arms up, waving and yelling. This went on until we were well beyond the reach of bullets. The stewardesses seemed to be enjoying it almost as much as we were.

It was a fourteen-hour flight to the refueling point, Anchorage, Alaska. Then a shorter hop down to Fort Lewis, in Washington state. The whole trip took twenty hours. It was the morning of March 23, 1969 when we finally arrived. From the air, Mount Rainier, with its snowy cap, looked absolutely magnificent. It was difficult to believe I would be standing on American soil again. When we disembarked the crisp, dry air was a wonderful shock to my lungs, long accustomed as they were to equatorial heat and humidity.

We were escorted to a large room, given an opportunity to re-enlist, and handed our separation orders. Then we were fed steak dinners, thanked for our service, and officially discharged. Buses took us to the Seattle-Tacoma airport. I caught a flight to

Dallas, then Austin later that afternoon. Before leaving Ft. Lewis I called mom and dad, and they were at the Austin airport to greet me, including Loopy.

How good it was to behold their beaming faces. And how strange it was to see the sights of home, to walk the streets and not hear artillery, or angry jets overhead, loaded with bombs to drop on other humans; to sleep where it is safe and comfortable, where there is family love. Several months passed before living in peace felt normal again.

EPILOGUE

Not long after coming home, I contacted Mailee. We wrote and spoke by phone many times while we attended school, she in Thailand, me in Austin. I worked at the university clinic and other nursing jobs to pay the bills. Two years passed before I proposed to her, after attaining a measure of financial security. We met in Hawaii once, and there made arrangements with our two governments for her to apply for US citizenship. She came to Texas and we married in the spring of 1971. We decided to finish medical school together, and eventually earned doctor's degrees. Then we established a family practice in a little town not far from Austin. A year and a half after we were married, Mailee gave birth to a girl. Three years later, a boy. They now have grown children of their own who have started families. They live not far away.

It wasn't until January 11, 2018 that the Guardian Angels declared it was time to publish this story. I'd worked on it during rare, idle hours, writing and re-writing, for almost fifty years. My Guardians visited during sleep many times over those five decades, always offering editorial advice and refreshing my memory. Though they always refused to offer more revelations.

I very much look forward to seeing and working with them during waking hours on the mansion worlds. It shouldn't be that long until I resurrect in that new and young body. This Earthly body is about used up. I've had my three-score and ten, and then some.

What a life it's been, rich as well as challenging, and always unpredictable. While in Nam, I wasn't sure life would last this long. But after listening to, and learning from, my Guardians, it didn't really matter how long life might be. Because of their abiding presence, and the things they revealed, I realized everyone has Guardian Angels, also a future life, if they so choose. And that everyone will someday become aware of their Guardians, if not on Earth, then on God's mansion worlds.